What the critics are saying:

I've got to admit, this story had me from the moment it started.... Diana Hunter has truly out done herself with this book....Kudos for crafting a story that makes one want to take a step out of the normal in our lives and experience something a bit more. - *Cyn Witkus, In The Library Reviews*

I enjoyed reading Table For Four; it's an intriguing story, with twist and turns that will titillate, capture your attention and hold it till the end. If you haven't read any of Ms. Hunter's work run out a get it you won't be disappointed. -*Susan Holly, Just Erotic Romance Reviews*

Discover for yourself why readers can't get enough of the multiple award-winning publisher Ellora's Cave. Whether you prefer e-books or paperbacks, be sure to visit EC on the web at www.ellorascave.com for an erotic reading experience that will leave you breathless.

www.ellorascave.com

TABLE FOR FOUR
An Ellora's Cave Publication, July 2004

Ellora's Cave Publishing, Inc.
PO Box 787
Hudson, OH 44236-0787

ISBN #1-84360-952-5

ISBN MS Reader (LIT) ISBN #1-84360-911-8
Other available formats (no ISBNs are assigned):
Adobe (PDF), Rocketbook (RB), Mobipocket (PRC) & HTML

Edited by *Pamela Campbell*.
Cover art by *Syneca*.

To my dear husband for his patience

TABLE FOR FOUR

Diana Hunter

Chapter 1

The sounds of kids playing in the park across the street filtered in through the open balcony door and Lissa held still, listening. Playful screams tore the quiet of the afternoon as little girls slid down the slide in innocence and fun. A crack split the air and boy's voices shouted as one of their number started his trek around the bases. Two houses away, the noise of a lawnmower started up. That would be Mr. Philbee doing his weekly walk with the mowing monster he used to trim his scrap of a yard.

Sunlight indirectly filled the room where Melissa lay bound. The balcony was a southern exposure, but the overhanging roof kept the rays from falling directly into the bedroom. The four-poster bed with its high, wrought iron columns, sat squarely against the western wall; soon the westering sun would fall upon her naked body, making her full bosom glow red in the long rays that filtered through the wisps of cloud.

Was there anything better than this? Lying bound in bed while life teemed around her? The scent of Mr. Philbee's freshly mown grass wafted in on the breeze and her nipples rose to meet it, almost as if they, too, could enjoy the fragrance. Melissa breathed deeply, loving the scent, the noise, and the bondage.

Just for the fun of it, she squirmed on the bed, enjoying her helplessness. She lay on her back, her arms over her head; her wrists hugged by Velcro cuffs and fastened to the swirls of the iron headboard. Her legs were spread wide, each one fastened via a cuff to a post of the bed. Although a little heavier than in her younger years, her lithe body was still trim and fit. The moving sun now tipped her nipples with fire and she arched her back to let the warmth caress her breasts even as the breeze blew a cooling draft across them.

Melissa loved bondage. She loved how the bindings felt on her skin, how their tightness constricted her movements. The thrill of being helpless, open to whatever whim her husband might desire.

David was out there now, doing yard work somewhere below the balcony. She imagined him trimming the bushes, or pruning the roses, or perhaps he was weeding the vegetables. He wasn't a tall man, so if he were trimming the bushes, he would be on the ladder, leaning precariously over the hedges to clip the branches in the back. At five foot ten, his height was perfect for pruning the rose climbers, his neat hands encased in heavy work gloves to protect them from the thorns. And if he were weeding the garden, his shirt would be wet from his perspiration, sticking to his lean frame as he knelt in the dirt. His short blond hair, damp around the temples from the afternoon sun, would hang in little waves of gold to frame his handsome patrician face.

Lissa knew that, no matter what task he had set himself, her blue-eyed husband wouldn't be far, because his overactive imagination worried about all sorts of terrible things happening to her when he stepped away. That made being helpless just a little less fun than it could be. Only in the past few months had she convinced him that she would be just fine and he didn't need to hover over her. But David had read all sorts of horror stories on the web about safe bondage and believed in them completely.

He even purchased a baby monitor and insisted on using it when he left her, carrying its mate with him in case she cried out. While the sane side of her admitted the practicality of such safety devices, her soul cried out for danger.

Because David was careful, he bound her in Velcro, not leather restraints with metal locks. The light cuffs fastened to the bed with old ties, not chains. David was cheap as well as safe. "It's just a fun game, Lissa," he told her over and over. "We can't afford to do like those pictures on the web. I bought you the four-poster, didn't I?"

Melissa and David had been married seven years, and Lissa knew she had pushed him as far as he would go. David was a traditional kind of guy and so, while they had done some pretty heavy petting before the wedding ceremony, the two of them were not *intimate*, as her mother referred to the sex act, until the wedding night. Lissa often brought up the subject of bondage both before and after the wedding; David always grinned at her and told her if that was what she wanted, he would be happy to give it to her.

But it was a game to him, and Lissa knew it after the first six months of their marriage. She was serious about it—vanilla sex just did not turn her on. Besides which, David did not have nearly the sexual appetite his earlier petting had led her to believe. From the first, sex was a Saturday night affair, and that was all.

In desperation, she had begged him to tie her up. The very act of begging had excited her so much that when he promised to do so the next Saturday, she came for the very first time in the midst of their plain old, ordinary sex.

David had been hesitant the next weekend—he didn't really know how to tie knots—they didn't have any equipment. He had many excuses. So Lissa raided the clothesline for the rope. But then, on top of it all, David giggled through most of the attempt. It had been an exercise in frustration.

Lissa then embarked on a study of bondage, because she had to admit, while the thought of being bound excited her and fueled her fantasies, she really didn't know much about the topic. The Internet opened a completely new world to her and she spent several months bookmarking the best sites she found in order to share her ideas with David. Communication was the key, she convinced herself as she performed her wifely duties each Saturday night.

And so, armed with knowledge, she approached him again several months after that first try. Bemused, David skimmed through some of the sites as Lissa sat beside him on the floor. He thought it was because the other chair was too far away; she wanted to pretend she was his slave. But he was not ready for that step yet. Lissa understood David needed to be trained to be a Master, and she would just take it one step at a time.

Except you can't change a chicken into a fox. David still insisted on his sex every Saturday night the way he'd always gotten it. Lissa finally suggested that he bind her in someway prior to the sex and that would be foreplay for her. Then he could untie her and they would have sex as normal. The suggestion saved her sanity. Over the years she taught him several different positions and slowly introduced a few toys into their play. But leather and chains were too much for David—and too expensive.

Lissa knew they could afford it, except there were always other priorities for the money. First the two of them bought the house, then of course, there were the repairs that needed to be made, then the decorating move from early garage sale to low-budget first-hand furniture. Each step moved them up in the world, made their lives prettier, giving the signs that all was well with them as they moved up the twin ladders of success and prosperity.

And, if the truth were told, Lissa would happily admit that David was a wonderful partner in every other way. She appreciated his thoughtfulness, his willingness to share the household tasks, even the fact that he took care of her. Only in the bedroom did Lissa find fault with her husband.

Of course, David had tied her very well today. Although the restraints were Velcro, Lissa still couldn't get them undone. She had already tried. That was part of the fun. Early on, David would leave her an out, and Lissa always found it sooner than she wanted to. With the use of the baby monitor, she had convinced him she didn't need the out—she could call if she needed him. So today, David had tied the bindings tight and walked away.

The sun was almost down and her breasts now dimmed in shadow. Lissa heard several mothers yell for their children, collect them and pass by the balcony on their way home. Her own stomach growled in reply and a moment later, she heard her husband in the shower; it was his ritual to shower after the day's labor and before they had sex. Most of her liked his consideration; only a small part wanted his sweaty, smelly body pressed against her, as she lay, unable to stop him. Knowing he was near and that soon the weight of his body would be upon her, dampness grew between her legs. And when the breeze blew over her pussy, she gasped in pleasure and squirmed in her bindings. Any moment David would walk through the door of their bedroom, unbind her and take her — missionary style.

The thought almost caused her juices to dry up. She could fantasize all she wanted; the truth was, it would never be different. Angrily she pulled on the bindings that, a few moments earlier, had given her such pleasure. A small cry of frustration strangled in her throat as she bit back the tears.

The door to the bath opened and she heard him padding his way to the bedroom. But his steps took a detour and she knew he was checking the email in the study. Taking a deep breath, she steadied herself and when David finally entered the room, her smile was warm, inviting, and sexy. In spite of her sexual frustration, she still loved him very much.

David Patterson looked at his wife, spread wide on the bed, her smile inviting him to play with her pert breasts and hard pencil-eraser nipples. She waggled them at him, and he grinned as the roundness of her breasts, somewhat flattened by her position on her back, bounced from side to side. Her dark brown hair lay tousled on the pillow creating a halo with her shoulder-length tresses. And further down, her open pussy glistened in the last of the evening light, just waiting to be satisfied. The entire time he had been out puttering in the yard, he thought of her waiting for him — except he knew he was bound to disappoint her again, no pun intended.

Of course, the feeling was mutual. This bondage thing just didn't do anything for him. He eyed her critically as she continued her "come-hither" look and knew the sight of a beautiful woman bound and helpless was a dream many men wanted all their lives—and didn't get. But he just wanted a woman to love and to hold, and if they had sex that was fine and if they didn't, well, that was fine, too.

He had tried to accommodate her, but as was true of all compromises, neither of them was completely happy. Still, he would go through the motions just to please her and for no other reason than because he loved her.

"And how is my vixen? Tired of her bondage?" David let his love for his wife shine in his eyes as he removed the towel from his waist. His cock was not yet erect, but Lissa knew well when it was, it would be long and slender—he could do so much with a cock like that if he would only try!

Melissa knew the drill. "Yes, David, would you release me now?" Her soul longed to call him Master or at the very least, Sir, but he would never allow it. And to be honest, he had never earned the right. He was her equal in all things.

"Of course, sweetheart." Methodically, he untied her, starting with her left wrist, then ankle; moving around the bottom of the bed, he untied her right ankle then wrist. Lissa massaged her own arms while he loosened the muscles in her legs. This had been one of her longer sessions and he worried about her muscles cramping, but Lissa never complained.

Her pussy ached for his touch as his hands kneaded her thigh. Mentally, she willed him higher. Her hands, driven by her awakening need, slipped from her arms to her breasts, massaging them and rolling the nipples in her fingers. Lissa purred and arched her back, giving him, literally, an open invitation.

David complied. Over the years he had learned how to touch her to make her come. His own cock, soft when he emerged from his shower, now grew as he moved closer to what would happen after Lissa came.

His fingers slid along her slit and Lissa moaned. David didn't have a lot of staying power, so he had settled on this pattern for sex over a year ago. First he would help her to her orgasm, then he would enter her and come in a few moments. Total time for the actual sex act? About ten minutes.

That was one of the reasons Lissa asked to be bound. In the past, when they tried to come together, she was always left in the cold. He would be done and then not have the energy to help her along. Most Saturday nights back then, she went to bed frustrated, determined to find some time the next day to take care of matters herself.

But the switch had been his idea; Lissa gave him a lot of credit for that. It had happened when she finally had the courage to tell him about her bondage fantasies. By tying her up and walking away, Lissa could let her imagination soar. By the time David returned, she was hot, wet, and ready to come in seconds.

It had been taking longer and longer, however. Today, she was only mildly stimulated and it took David quite a while to produce the desired effect. He wouldn't use his mouth — that was one of his taboos. But his fingers played and poked and pinched and soon Lissa felt the familiar tension build between her legs to release a moment later, her pussy lips contracting around David's fingers.

"All done?" he asked with a smile. She smiled weakly and nodded — let him think it was because it was earth-shattering rather than the mild, soft orgasm that it had been.

David now parted her legs and Lissa obediently spread them wide, bringing her knees to her chest to give him better access. Never once in their seven years of marriage, had she come on her back. All those women in the few porn videos they'd rented out of curiosity must've been faking it, she decided. There was absolutely nothing sexy about this position.

Her pussy was so warm and tight, even after all these years, and David loved having his slender cock inside it. For a moment, he teased himself, hovering just outside her opening, rubbing along the length with his hand and making the veins stand out. In the last video they watched together, the actress had given several magnificent blowjobs, but David could never ask Lissa to do such a thing to him — it was too demeaning and she was his wife.

Imagining that unknown actress kneeling before him, he plunged into Lissa's pussy the way he wanted to take that woman's mouth. He grunted as the pressure built, then exploded inside his wife's pussy, with images of another woman's face before him.

He pulled out and grabbed for a few tissues before rolling onto his side. Lissa had several in her hand already and she wiped his spilled seed from her pussy before it ran out and made a mess of the sheets. David appreciated her gesture — she was lying on his side of the bed and he really didn't want to sleep in that mess later.

His stomach growled. "Come on, my sexy lazybones, let's go out to dinner, since you didn't make anything for my supper!" His teasing smile took any offense out of his rebuke.

Lissa grinned and stretched. Okay, so David wasn't great in bed — he was wonderful in every other way.

* * * * *

A small diner just down the street and around the corner from their modest house tended to be one of their habitual eating spots. Their usual booth by the front picture window was available and Lissa and David slid in along the maroon vinyl seats facing each other across the matching maroon table.

They ordered and David told her what he'd accomplished while she was "busy" elsewhere. He was very careful not to refer to her private fetish in public — to do so would violate another taboo. Lissa, however, was grateful for his discretion, it had taken her a long time to tell the person she most loved in all the world; there was no way she wanted anyone else to know.

Indeed, part of the arousal of the afternoon was listening to the life teeming around her; life that had no idea what little secret lay behind the open balcony door just above their heads.

The diner filled quickly and when the little bell over the door rang again, David looked up as something or someone caught his eye — and stared. Lissa frowned and nudged his foot under the table, but it seemed to have no effect. Turning her head slightly, she saw what held his fascination.

A man and a woman had entered and were making their way down the aisle toward them. With her straight, long blonde hair and svelte figure, the woman was a walking goddess. Her dark heels were at least six inches high — which just about matched the length of her navy blue skirt.

But while Lissa acknowledged the beauty of the woman, it was the man who followed that held her eye.

Even though the woman's heels made her tall, the male behind her still towered a full head above her, his broad chest and commanding bearing daring Lissa to look away. His neatly trimmed wavy black hair fell in small curls just long enough to give a girl something to run her fingers through. His round face sported a small goatee and neatly trimmed mustache. The very image of a Gypsy king come to life.

The diner was full and every eye watched the couple as they made their way along the narrow aisle. No seats were left and when the waitress apologized and told them they'd have to wait, the gentleman, without turning his gaze from Lissa, told the server in a smooth voice, "That won't be necessary. I'm sure this nice couple will share their booth with us, will you not?"

There was a faint accent in his quiet, baritone voice, but Lissa could not place it. She tore her eyes away to signal "no!" to David, but he was already moving over and letting the woman slide in next to him. The blonde made an odd little movement, then settled next to Lissa's husband and smiled across the table at her. Lissa smiled weakly in return, while glaring at her husband. What was he doing?

"Please, by all means. We are happy to share the table." David tore his eyes away from the blonde beauty just long enough to dismiss the waitress. But anything further was cut off as he watched the goddess readjust her seat, and flip up her short skirt to place her naked rear end on the vinyl seat cover. He knew he was ogling, but he just couldn't stop. It wasn't every day that a beautiful woman just walked into your life and showed you her ass.

David's entranced absorption of the blonde goddess' actions made her male companion smile. He watched his partner and when her soft blue eyes met his and she nodded, he knew she wanted to play. While he spoke English extremely well, he let his rich baritone affect more of an accent than usual as he made his apologies to the couple whose booth they had invaded.

"Thank you, sir, you have saved my lovely Adora from having to stand so long in her shoes. They make her sexy, do they not?" He put out his left hand and Lissa caught sight of a large gold signet ring on his forefinger — but no wedding band a little further along. The woman he called Adora smiled at him and placed her hand in his. The image of her slender and delicate hand in his larger and rougher one made Lissa's heart skip a beat as she recognized their poetic contrast: he was night, she was day.

David's mouth was dry and he hurriedly sipped from his water glass to cover the fact that this man's girlfriend had given him a hard-on—an amazing accomplishment, considering he had just had sex with his wife not an hour before. "Yes," he finally managed. "Yes, her shoes, I mean, your shoes are very sexy." He tried not to look down, but the woman's tight shirt barely covered her bosom and her cleavage just cried out to for a quick glance.

"Oh, David, really!" scolded Lissa, totally embarrassed by her husband's obvious fascination with the blonde, but more embarrassed by her own internal reactions to the man beside her. Her panties were soaked and her pussy was open and aching, right there in the restaurant. For crying out loud, she was a married woman!

"Methinks my Adora likes your husband's attentions, even as you are not sure you appreciate mine, my dear woman. Permit me to introduce myself. I am Master Richard."

If the man were not sitting so close to her and so obviously exuding sex appeal all over the place, Lissa might have laughed at the Hollywood movie tone the man affected. And what was up with the Master title? All the man needed was an opera cape with red satin lining and the picture would be complete. He already was dressed in the suit. All right, so he wasn't wearing a white tie and tails, but a nice three-piece, well-cut, black, very sexy suit.

His left hand occupied with Adora, Richard now held out his right to Lissa, palm up in a gesture of peace. He noted how the woman beside him shrank away, careful to not touch him with any part of her body, and waited until she extended her own hand, noting she was unable, or unwilling, to meet his eyes. Master Richard gently took her hand in his, turning it and bringing it to his lips. The kiss on the back of her hand intentionally put her off balance.

Lissa knew she should not sit here and hold hands with a perfect stranger, no matter how sexy he was. Even knowing she should pull her hand away, she remained still, letting him touch her.

"Pleased to meet you," she murmured, more out of habit than real pleasure.

Richard decided to let the pretty dark-haired woman off the hook, turning to the gentleman across from her. "Sir, you have met Adora, my beloved. And I have introduced myself. Is it not the custom for you to now introduce your wife and yourself?" There was a hint of amusement in his voice, since the man was still entranced with his companion.

"Oh! Erm, yes, of course." David cleared his throat and shook his head, trying desperately to bring his mind back under control and focus on something other than the extremely sexy woman beside him. "I'm David Patterson, and this is my wife, Lissa."

"Enchanted." Richard released Adora's hand, but still held Lissa's; he turned it over to place a tender kiss on her palm. His eyes held hers, never leaving her face; Lissa felt her soul was open to the man's inspection. An absurd thought ran through her head that perhaps the man really was the King of the Gypsies and she smiled at the absurdity.

"Ah! Your lady smiles and the world lights with happiness."

The waitress brought their dinners and saved Lissa further embarrassment. Her cheeks burning a bright pink, she withdrew her hand to take her dinner plate from the waitress' hand. Since the new arrivals had not yet ordered, the server now turned her attention to the handsome couple. Richard's voice was different when he spoke to the waitress; he ordered for the two of them in clipped tones that brooked no nonsense. It occurred to Lissa that she had yet to hear the woman speak.

As the waitress hurried away and Master Richard turned his attention to David, Lissa tried to calm the heartbeat that thundered in her ears. What was it about the man beside her that caused her stomach to flutter as if she were a schoolgirl? Clearly David appreciated Adora, and Lissa knew that she should be jealous—he certainly hadn't looked at her like that in a very, very long time.

But as the two men spoke, Lissa found she could not find it in her to be resentful. One might as well be jealous that one's lover appreciated the Venus d'Milo or one of Ruben's beauties. There was no denying the woman was as much a work of art as her male companion. Under her lashes, Lissa found her gaze pulled back to the man beside her time and time again. His high cheekbones fascinated her; subtle emotions played over his face, keeping her attention. Although not loud or boisterous, he dominated the conversation, turning it, guiding it along safe lines. She, herself, did not join in. Naturally shy by nature, she let David do the talking while she sat feeling awkward at the entire situation.

Adora also remained silent while the two men exchanged ideas and learned about each other. Lissa glanced at her now and again and more than once their eyes met. Each time, Lissa was favored with a friendly smile, but not a single word did the woman utter.

That wasn't to say the woman did not communicate. Adora actively listened to the conversation, often smiling at the men when one of them said something particularly clever or witty. When Master Richard started to order dessert for the two of them, she frowned and shook her head; her partner changed the order to reflect her wishes.

For his part, David found the man to be extremely well-educated, well-read, and well-spoken. The two had numerous interests in common; the theatre, art films, and tastes in books were all discussed and agreed upon. Richard did not seem to mind David's appreciation of his companion's beauty; and the attention Richard paid to Lissa made David feel grateful. It also lessened his feelings of guilt for his early blatant reaction. He did not notice Adora's reticence — only her smile when he said something that pleased her.

Finally, dinner and desserts consumed, the time came to depart. Lissa had been ready to leave for some time — the temperature in the diner had grown extremely warm. Too bad she and David had already had their Saturday night sex; she certainly needed to give vent to the arousal that had continued to build inside her all through dinner. She thought of herself as she had been earlier, spread upon the bed; open, wanting—only the man who walked through the door to release her was not her husband, but Master Richard.

She watched his graceful hands as he accepted his dinner bill from the waitress, well-kept, strong hands. Large and powerful. He wore only the one silver ring; his long fingers needed no other adornment. In her mind, she imagined those hands caressing her helpless body, playing with her as a cat plays with its food. Those fingers running along her spread arms, touching her breasts...

"Lissa. Lissa," David repeated. What was wrong with her? She'd been very quiet all through dinner, yet she hadn't seemed upset. Or was she mad at him for his attention to Adora? "Are you listening to me?"

"Yes, David, I'm right here." Lissa answered, her voice calm even though his question had jolted her from her erotic reverie. "I'm sorry, what did you ask me?" She brought her mind back to the present with a struggle.

"Do you have anything planned for Monday night?"

"No, neither of us have anything on the calendar." It was a running joke between the two of them—if a date was not on the calendar, it didn't exist. Both of them were very careful to inform the other of various appointments and commitments. The calendar served as another example of their neat and ordered lives.

"Fine, then. Richard, we will be there around six on Monday evening then."

"Be there? Be where?" Lissa mentally cursed her momentary lapse into daydreaming.

"Richard has invited us to join Adora and him for dinner at their place on Monday," David explained patiently.

"I trust, Madame Patterson, that is acceptable to you?" He made no attempt to hide the humor in his eyes; his careful questioning of her husband and her own reactions to him gave him the information he needed. Though her own silent signal, Adora had communicated to him her wishes in the matter; this couple had definite possibilities.

Master Richard had turned his gaze on her once more and again she felt the force of those dark eyes. This was totally *not* acceptable to her. She opened her mouth to protest when those long and sexy fingers closed over hers on her lap and her heart jumped into her throat, forestalling her objection.

"Please, Madame, be our guest. Adora would love your company."

Lissa's eyes sought out the woman, who gazed back at her with warmth and friendship. *Why don't you speak to me?* Lissa wanted to shout at her. David pushed his foot against his wife's leg and got Lissa's perturbed attention. He raised an eyebrow and nodded toward Adora with his head. Lissa understood. David wanted another opportunity to get an eyeful of the beautiful woman.

"Yes," Lissa finally replied, defeated and aware that Master Richard still held her hand. She shrank even further into the corner of the booth as she once again extricated herself from his touch. "Thank you for your invitation; we will be happy to visit with you for dinner." Her words were wooden and the malevolent glance she tossed in her husband's direction let David know the two of them would have it out when they got home.

Master Richard stood and Lissa breathed a little easier. The Gypsy King held out his hand to his Beautiful Lady, who accepted his gesture with grace as she stood and smoothed her short skirt. Without another word—or another look at Lissa or David—the couple paid their bill and left the diner. Lissa let out a sigh of relief that went to the very bottom of her toes.

"Well, thank goodness they've gone." She dropped her head in her hands and rubbed her temples. "How could you accept that invitation without asking me?"

David looked at her as if she had lost her mind. "Were you or were you not sitting right here at this table when he asked us? I tried to catch your attention, but you were off in la-la land or something. Just what were you looking at anyway?"

"His hands."

"His hands? You couldn't hear what was being said because you were watching his hands?"

The graceful way his hands moved through the air as he spoke, drawing his point in the space before him as if the atmosphere itself were his canvas. Those hands drawing on her body, melting her, molding her, taking her to places she only dreamed of.

"Yes," she snapped. "I was watching his hands. Sue me. At least I wasn't trying to undress him!" Her daydream hadn't gotten that far.

"Lissa, I think we'd best go home." David slid out of the booth with an air of finality.

"Fine." She knew she was being unreasonable. But how could she tell her husband, whom she loved so very deeply, that she was having a fantasy about another man?

* * * * *

They walked the few blocks to their home in silence. Darkness had fallen and although the neighborhood was a safe one, Lissa still held David's arm for protection. It deterred men from giving her a second glance when they realized she already belonged to someone. Many others were out enjoying the summer evening and she smiled and nodded to those they passed, glad for David's arm.

Usually David liked this walk home through the busy streets. Greeting both friend and neighbor was always a pleasant activity. Not so tonight. He was glad they met no one they knew, he didn't really want to be dragged into a long conversation about small talk. Not when his mind was still filled with images of a bare-assed blonde—and with an upset wife beside him.

"Lissa, come here." David gestured to the living room couch as soon as they entered their front door. "We need to talk about why you're so mad. Please?" he added when he saw her hesitation.

She never could resist that puppy dog look he got in his eyes when he wanted something. Acquiescing, she followed him to the couch and tucked a leg under so she could sit facing him. Crossing her arms, she waited for him to start.

"Dinner was very...interesting," David began, letting his voice trail off so Lissa would embellish, and enlighten him as to why she was angry.

"Interesting is a good word." She knew full well what he was doing and didn't feel in the mood to help him at all. He could fish all he wanted, she wasn't going to bite.

"Richard's smart and witty."

Lissa nodded. So far the ground was safe, but any conversation about the male half of the couple was bound to make her start blushing and then she'd tip her hand. Better to get David to talk. "But Adora didn't say a single word all evening, did you notice?"

"Well, you were pretty quiet as well, my dear heart. Don't think I didn't notice your own reticence."

Blast him, he'd turned the conversation neatly back to her own feelings—right where she didn't want to be. She tried again. "I wonder what type of voice she has—low and sultry? Or soft and sexy?"

David gave up. "All right, let's just talk about it, all right? I have no idea what her voice sounds like; I was too busy looking at her body. There. Are you satisfied?"

Lissa smiled. Bingo! Getting David to talk about Adora was much safer than bringing her male companion into the conversation. Tucking her own disquieting fantasies deep into her dreams, she endeavored to keep the conversation about her husband and his imaginings. Her voice took on a gentler tone. "David, I really don't mind that you ogled her body—how could you not? You're a red-blooded American male with distinctly good taste in beauty." She shrugged her shoulders. "If you hadn't responded, I would have been seriously concerned about your eyesight, and your libido!"

"So you don't mind that I had several impure thoughts about another woman?" David narrowed his eyes as he zeroed in on his target. In his heart, he knew she wasn't really angry, over the years the two of them had often pointed out objects of beauty to one another. No, her anger stemmed from something else that she didn't want to admit.

"No, I don't really mind that you found her attractive — she is a beautiful woman."

"And Richard certainly seemed to be a handsome man, don't you think?"

Lissa pulled her leg out from under her in an effort to hide her thoughts from her husband. "Yes," she stated, keeping her voice flat, "he is a handsome man." She sneered, "But what kind of man goes around calling himself Master Richard? Seems to me he was a bit full of himself, calling himself that!" Of course, there was one type of man who had that right. But even those in the "lifestyle" as they called it, didn't give that title out in public. Hours spent pouring over Internet sites, discovering she was not alone in wanting to be tied up, had also taught her something of the etiquette of Dominant/submissive relationships. A relationship she suspected their dinner companions shared. A relationship she would love to experience.

But David would never understand that, and she had no words to tell him. Instead she just frowned and shook her head. "Master, indeed!"

"He had an accent, perhaps where he comes from, that's the proper form of address, or maybe he's just not so familiar with modern American customs." David felt a need to defend the man with whom he'd just spent an enjoyable dinner. But he knew he was getting closer — was it her feminist leanings that made her dinner partner rub the wrong way?

Lissa rolled her eyes at David's suggestions. "I doubt either of those is true. I think he's a man who just likes to put on airs." Airs that caused her flesh to cry out for his touch. Airs that made her breath catch in her throat. She averted her gaze and fiddled with a newspaper on the coffee table so he would not read the truth in her eyes.

David stood. They would get nowhere tonight. Lissa had slammed up a wall and was not about to take it down while the reasons were so fresh. Maybe by morning she would have put everything into perspective and they could discuss it again.

"Well, dear, I'm sorry I got you into a dinner you do not want to attend. Won't you please go and just put up with him for one more evening? Then, if he doesn't make a better impression on you, I won't push it further." He held out his hand to help her to her feet.

"All right." He was making those puppy dog eyes at her again and Lissa knew when she was defeated. "But I'm taking you at your word. If I don't want to ever see them again after dinner Monday night, I don't have to. You and Master Richard can go off and do things on your own."

David laughed. "And perhaps you and Adora will become best friends!"

"Only if she learns how to talk!" Lissa shot back as they entered the bedroom.

"Perhaps you should not talk now," David whispered as he pulled his wife close to him, nuzzling his nose deep into her auburn hair, her spicy scent filling his senses as images of long blonde tresses swirled a net around his imagination.

To have sex twice on a Saturday night was unusual to say the least. But then, it had been an unusual Saturday dinner. Lissa did not complain when her husband's lips closed over hers emphasizing his desire for her silence. She inhaled his aftershave, letting the scent begin to carry her away even as her mind wondered what cologne a Gypsy king would wear.

David's hands ran over Lissa's body, loving how she felt; he knew every curve, every spot that produced a tickle—and every spot that would produce a moan. He wanted moans tonight. He needed to hear his wife respond to his touch as he imagined himself in bed with another.

His fingers unbuttoned her blouse even as hers trembled to unbutton his shirt. She pushed it off his shoulders and for once did not make any attempt to catch it and hang it neatly over the chair. Instead, she let it lie, pressing her lips to his nipple, sucking gently to make it stand up, hard and proud. David was not a hairy man and Lissa enjoyed running her tongue over his satiny smooth chest. *Did Richard have a smooth chest?* She doubted it and wondered what it would be like to run her fingers through a mat of hair on a hirsute man.

Their sexy dinner companions remained silent partners in their lovemaking as David undressed Lissa and led her to the bed. For David, the thought of actually having sex with another woman made making love to his own wife that much more sweet. Her fantasies of bondage aside, she was such an innocent lover. He pulled aside the covers for her and watched as she crawled into the bed from his side, her naked body gleaming in the moonlight from the still-opened shade. Standing beside the bed, he fantasized that the figure belonged to Adora and that she would turn and take his cock in her mouth. He ran his hand along its length as he indulged himself in the dream, then climbed into bed beside his wife.

David was a wonderful, careful lover, and Lissa knew how lucky she was to have him, even though she longed for a rougher touch. His hands cupped her breast as he carefully placed a kiss on her nipple sending a small shiver down her belly to her sex. She imagined him throwing his care for her to the wind and grabbing her hard. Her breath caught in her throat as she fancied Master Richard's ring glinting in the moonlight as the gypsy's fingers squeezed her breast. But it was the hand of her husband and in her guilt at wanting another man, she made love to David as if it were the first time, covering his neck and the hollow of his throat with her kisses.

Knowing Lissa had never come on her back, David entered her that way anyway, then swung her up and over his hip until she was seated on top, his long and slender cock firmly nestled inside her warm, wet opening. She squealed and giggled as his firm hands lifted her and the two of them switched positions. Her legs straddled his hips and she pushed herself upright, feeling the movement of his cock inside her.

"Mmmm, David. I like this position very much."

"I know you do. Now ride me, woman, and make your husband come!" David's voice was husky with desire and Lissa knew she shouldn't tease him. Not now. Not tonight.

Gripping him tightly with her vaginal muscles, a groan from below rewarded her. She leaned forward ever so slightly, just enough to get pressure onto her clit, and felt the familiar warm fuzzy feeling radiate outward as she connected. Many Saturdays, David's careful handling of her meant she didn't come, but with the image of Richard's hands on her body swirling through her head, the tension built quickly. Her breath grew more and more ragged as David pumped into her from below.

Lissa rarely made any noise during sex—David knew she was quiet by nature. But tonight she whimpered and even cried out once as her orgasm moved closer to reality. Until he heard her cries, he had not realized he missed them. She used to cry out much more often when they were first married—only in the past year had she grown quiet. Quiet like Adora. Hearing her moans fueled his own need and as he joined her in the riding of their bodies, he imagined himself making a certain blonde woman scream her climax.

For the first time in ages, they came together, the music of their passion louder than it had been in many, many years. And when Lissa collapsed on top of him, David held her close, loving how she snuggled into him for warmth and protection. He could not remember a time when he'd felt so close to her.

"Lissa..." he whispered. She said nothing, but simply turned her head so she could see him in the moonlight, and he continued, his thoughts unguarded after their moment of passion. "Lissa, have you ever dreamed of being with another man?"

Lissa smiled sadly at her husband—he must have known. "Yes, but not often!" She didn't want him to think her fantasies often got away with her.

"I do, too," he admitted. "I mean, I think of being with another woman, not another man." David grinned—he liked women way too much to care about sex with a man. In fact, having more than one woman service him would be just fine. "But it doesn't mean I don't love you," he hastened to add.

"Of course it doesn't, silly!" Lissa giggled. "No more than appreciating a fine figure walking down the street means you no longer find me attractive." She paused for effect. "You do still find me attractive, don't you?"

"You're beautiful." David kissed her nose for emphasis, then let his head fall back to the pillow, staring up at the ceiling as his thoughts continued to spin. "I know I cannot give you all you need in bed..." His voice trailed off, unsure how to suggest what he was thinking.

"David, you have tried the dominance-thing and it isn't for you. That's okay. It means a lot to me that you tried." Lissa hugged him close to her so he would not see the longing in her eyes. She loved him and would not hurt him for the world. But as long as they were being honest, there was a piece that she should own up to. "And I know I am not exactly the lover you would like either," she murmured into his chest.

David kissed the top of her head. "You are my wife, and I respect you. I guess it would be nice to be with a woman I didn't have to respect. Just once," he added as her head came up to look at him. "Just once, that's all. It's just a fantasy, anyway." He tried not to sound defensive.

"You do respect me, and that's what we both need from each other. A *mutual* respect." Lissa stressed the word mutual — trying to make him realize they both had unfulfilled fantasies. "And David, that's all right. I want your respect in our relationship. She paused, then added quietly, "I just don't want your respect in the bedroom."

"What, you want me to treat you like a tramp?" David shook his head. "I can't do that. I love you too much."

"I know. But yes, just once in *my* life I want to be a slut. I want to have sex that's down and dirty and rough." When he said nothing, she looked up at him, nervous that she had said too much. "I've shocked you, haven't I?"

David shook his head. "Actually, you haven't, and that's what surprises me. I guess I've known that for some time. Are you disappointed that I can't give that to you?"

Lissa shrugged and held him tighter. "Only a little," she admitted. "Are you disappointed that I can't give you what you want?"

For answer, David returned her hug. "Only a little." He pulled her up to him and kissed her long and deep, her lips all the sweeter for the revelations she made. "Get some sleep, my love."

Lissa's smile was fond as she rolled over to her side of the bed. In moments, David's soft snores filled the room, but Lissa stared at the wall, her mind filled with guilt and images of a tall man with broad shoulders, dressed all in black. It was quite some time before exhaustion pulled her into a restless sleep.

Chapter 2

All too quickly Monday evening was on her doorstep.

Over the intervening forty-eight hours, she and David had shied away from the topic they had discussed Saturday night. Their mutual admission of dissatisfaction with each other's sexual styles created an intimacy neither expected. An intimacy fragile and precious. Neither one wanted to break it.

Still, when Lissa didn't emerge from her shower for over an hour late Monday afternoon, David's patience was sorely tried. "What took you so long? It's only a diner date with friends."

"Yeah, well, shaving takes time, you know!" Lissa shot over her shoulder as she rummaged through her closet. But once she heard the bathroom door shut and knew she was alone again, she leaned her forehead against the clothes bar and tried to still her thoughts that ran as out of control as a flock of chickens when the fox was near.

Just why *was* she primping so much for this dinner? Every time David had mentioned their dinner date, Lissa rolled her eyes and shook her head. But now, in the darkness of her closet, with David's words ringing in her head, she faced the awful truth about the dinner she was about to attend. She was afraid.

Master Richard's face, his voice, his touch on her hand, haunted her every waking moment. To see him again was something she wanted more than anything. She imagined him commanding her, tying her up and using her body as a toy. She imagined him caressing her face and her breasts with his hands, while she offered her body for his pleasure.

But even as her mind touched on the thought, she recoiled. She could not look so deep, what lay hidden there only brought her shame and sent a spike of fear through her stomach. All day she had been on edge and hadn't eaten a thing. Now she was very glad she hadn't. To desire such a thing almost made her physically ill. It was too perverted — she must banish such thoughts from her mind.

She finished dressing and eyed the bottom drawer of her dresser. Makeup or no makeup? Usually it was too much to bother with, although David liked to see her wear it when they went out. Personally, she preferred to show her real face to the world — not some mask she put on. Cringing at her own hypocrisy, she turned from the dresser in disgust.

Pulling faces at himself in the mirror as he shaved off the day's growth, David grinned at the irony. Lissa was right, shaving did take time when you wanted to do it right. He had no illusions about accepting the invitation to dinner; while he enjoyed Richard's conversation, he really wanted another chance to admire Adora's beauty and fuel his fantasies. Forcing Lissa to endure the attentions of Master Richard seemed a small price to pay for one more glimpse of that erotic goddess.

By the time David emerged from his shower, Lissa had dressed and gone downstairs. And so he did not see the agonizing choices she made over each article of clothing. "Casual." That's how David had told her to dress for this evening. But "casual" meant so many different things depending on the situation. The weather forecaster predicted continuing warm weather, so Lissa finally decided on an ankle-length white skirt that buttoned up the side and a scoop-necked peasant blouse of pale pink. Scarlet red was her best color, but tonight was a night of subtlety...and desire. The critical glance she ran over her image in the large bedroom mirror turned faraway when it fell on the buttons that fastened her skirt. So easy for his strong hands to undo those buttons—one by one—until she lay bared to his sight. Only a small thong covered her pussy, the thin strap neatly dividing her cheeks and allowing no line to show through the white material. Lissa felt slutty and sexy; in the privacy of her house, she gave her hips a nice swing as she went downstairs.

But once they turned into the drive, Lissa's second thoughts clamored in her head. Khaki pants and a lightweight short-sleeve shirt were all well and good for David; men were so lucky. She didn't want lines, so she wore the thong; she wanted to look sexy, so she wore the pushup bra. And now that she was here, she wanted to run home and find a long-sleeved turtleneck sweater and a nice pair of baggy, unflattering sweatpants.

David's heartbeat raced with nervous excitement as the two of them managed the short walk to the front door. He wasn't sure what kind of house he had expected but there was a great deal of comfort in seeing the story-and-a-half Cape Cod tucked in among all the other "normal" houses on the street. Something unique—just like Adora.

He rang the doorbell and almost instantly, the goddess herself appeared at the door. Golden hair caught up in the back accentuated her naked, slender neck. Not even a necklace graced that whiteness. David could not stop his glance from traveling down to take in her beautiful bosom, barely contained in the tight tank top that stretched itself so thinly across her breasts he could see her nipples outlined against the light fabric. She again wore a skirt, a long, shimmering, sheer skirt this time that hid nothing. Nothing. Not A Thing. Only a nudge from Lissa brought him back to the fact that Richard had joined Adora at the door.

Dressed again all in black, the Gypsy king's regal bearing was impossible to ignore. Like a crown prince of Arabia, he bowed his greeting with a nod of his head and a graceful wave of his arm. "Welcome to our home." The deep sexiness of his voice, gentle and seductive, gave Lissa's stomach a little flip of excitement. Swallowing hard and raising her chin in defiance of her nervousness, she crossed the threshold and concentrated instead on the safer form of Adora as she followed her hostess into the house.

The entryway wasn't much more than an alcove in the corner of the house, a place more for keeping out the drafts in the winter than for any other useful purpose. A few steps brought them to the living room, exotically decorated with tapestries, two overstuffed armchairs and pillows.

Huge orange pillows with tassels.

Long bolster-type pillows of scarlet and black.

Thick, downy pillows, comfortable and alluring.

Their bright oranges and reds accentuated the deep rich blues and greens of the heavy, dark drapes hung at the windows. Many-hued tapestries covered the walls, pooling fabric on the floor in puddles of rich color. Several small lamps on tiny tables spilled soft, romantic light over the room.

For a moment, David and Lissa just gazed in astonishment before Lissa blurted, "It looks like the inside of a Gypsy caravan!"

"Ah, yes, my dear, a little bit of the Old Country here in our own home." Master Richard came up beside her, his hand on her elbow. Lissa resisted the urge to pull away, instead opting for a strong and steady look into the man's eyes. It was a mistake. Deep pools of quiet command gazed back at her, capturing her eyes, holding her soul in his gaze. Not since she was a teenager had Lissa blushed so deeply. She barely knew this man, why did he have the power to make her feel like an innocent schoolgirl? Her inner being naked before his scrutiny, Lissa found it difficult to breathe.

"Perhaps Madam would care to recline?"

Before she could protest, Master Richard led her to a luxurious pile of cushions beside one of the chairs. Determined to regain her composure, she avoided his eyes and sat with a graceful flourish of her skirt, being sure to let the slit in the side show just a bit of her calf and knee as she settled herself. Only then did she dare look at her husband.

David, however, was not paying her any attention. From the moment Adora slid her hand in his, he was aware of nothing but her wide blue eyes that spoke volumes to him. When she led him to the chair beside Lissa, he made no objection, willing to go anywhere the goddess led him.

While his outward demeanor remained amiable, Richard's inner self noted Lissa's careful dressing and

David's eagerness. The woman would not be easy; he could see she would be the one who needed convincing. And would the man still be interested in Adora once he knew some of her history? Richard eyed the couple carefully as they settled into settings very unfamiliar to them. He and Adora had searched before. Would these two be any different? Adora signaled him with a glance and he bowed to his guests.

"Be comfortable, my friends. We will return in a moment." Master Richard left the room, Adora following behind.

An arched opening stretched between the living room and dining room; Richard and Adora passed through it and turned right on the other side to disappear through a swinging door to the kitchen. To David, it seemed the light dimmed in the room when Adora followed her husband through the arch.

"So why do you suppose you get the chair and I get the floor? Don't tell me there aren't some very 'Old Country' traditions going on here!"

David forced himself to focus on his wife, still sitting gracefully among the cushions. "Can't say as I mind it." He grinned to let her know he was only teasing.

"Well, it's not all that uncomfortable." Lissa's concession was grudging. She grinned up at her husband. "You really are smitten, you know."

David sighed. There was no use trying to hide it. "I know. Are you mad?"

Lissa shook her head, a little surprised to discover she wasn't. "No, I'm not angry at all. She's gorgeous. I don't know if I've ever seen such a sexual being in my life." *Except for Master Richard,* she amended in her head.

"Really? That surprises me." Somehow he had not expected Lissa to respond to Adora's sex appeal.

"Why? Because I can see her erotic-ness? If there is such a word. She's the type of woman men fall all over themselves for. I can't be jealous of that. It's like being jealous of someone because they have a goatee and you do not."

"Like Richard's. Do you like his beard?"

David saw his wife's sudden discomfiture and knew he had hit closer to home than she wanted him to. "You're as smitten with him as I am with Adora!"

"No, I'm not!" But her cheeks colored and she looked away, pretending to examine the room's furnishings.

"Yes, you are! Admit it, Lissa. I know the man is sexy…heck, even I saw the way every woman's head turned in the diner. You blush every time he looks at you."

"Okay, so I find him a bit…attractive. But I still think he's a bit full of himself."

"Lissa, it's all right to admit you're attracted to him. In fact…" David hesitated.

"What?"

David searched her upturned face, so innocent, yet so full of life and desire. He knew his wife well, better than she thought he did. He knew she yearned for a sexual partner who would give her what she needed; what he could not. Was Master Richard that partner?

"In fact, I love you very much." He could not bring himself to suggest it. She would never consider such a thing. No matter how much he might want Adora.

The reply died on her lips as Master Richard reentered the room, his presence filling the empty spaces. Briefly,

Lissa ignored him, trying to determine what David had not said. Except the Gypsy king held out his hand in a regal gesture to help her rise.

"May I assist you, Madam? Our dinner is ready."

Determined to show this Old Country male that she wasn't as helpless as he wanted her to be, she almost batted away his hand in irritation. Why did he bring out such conflicting emotions in her? She couldn't decide if she wanted to submit to him, or deck him.

David's eyes were on her, a warning implicit in his gaze. With a sweet smile, Lissa gracefully placed her hand in Master Richard's. "Why, thank you, sir. What a gentleman you are." She could not help the southern accent that dripped from her voice. If Master Richard caught the sarcasm, his face betrayed no trace of it.

His tug on her hand, however, drove the sarcasm from her attitude. With a flourish, he literally pulled her to her feet; a move Lissa did not expect. Off balance, she leaned into his arm with a startled exclamation.

"Steady, my dear woman. You weigh so little! I should not have pulled you so fast."

She bit back a sharp retort as his eyes once again caught hers. The twinkle in them belied his apology. His move had been a deliberate calculation to put her in her place after her sarcasm. She knew it. But those eyes, those dark and sexy eyes that held no malice, pulled her in and even as he tucked her hand under his arm to lead her to dinner, Lissa's heart melted just a bit more.

Dinner was a Hungarian dish David could not pronounce, although Lissa did a credible job of getting the accent right. Again the primary conversation centered between the two men; Lissa spoke only a little and Adora not at all.

Once dinner ended, David and Richard left the women to the clean-up and walked outside to enjoy the summer night. David had been raised where everyone did their fair share; he knew Lissa would have a great deal to say about the stereotypical division of labor in this household. But the beautiful Adora worked to clean up his supper dishes behind that swinging door, and perhaps Lissa would learn something useful about the golden goddess that she could pass on to him. After giving his wife a warning glance, he walked out to enjoy the summer night with his companion.

"My father would often retire for a cigar after dinner. Always outside, my mother would not let him smoke inside." Richard chuckled. "He ruled the house with an iron fist, until Mama overruled him."

David laughed. "Not much different from my parents then. Whenever we kids had a problem that required parental involvement, we always went to Mom first, who then helped us figure out how to go to Dad."

"Then our families are much the same. Not so, Adora's." The dark man nodded toward the kitchen window where David could just see a glimpse of the room. A shadow passed in front of the curtain and David's heart jumped a bit, recognizing Adora's figure.

"How was hers different?"

For a moment, Richard was silent. The information he was about to impart had driven men away on more than one occasion. David, however, seemed a more open-minded soul. Richard hoped he was correct; the man's conversation at dinner showed him to be obviously well-educated, if not well-traveled. And Richard had seen the look in Adora's eyes; that haunted look she covered up when they met someone new. How many more times could her heart be broken? Better to find out now if David was worth any more of her time. He gave David a meaningful glance, narrowing his eyes as he took the man's measure. "Adora traveled a great deal with her family. Many places, some that did not welcome her kind."

David's head swiveled around. "Her kind? I don't understand."

"She is Roma."

"So?"

"Do you know what Roma are?"

David shook his head. Something told him the word didn't mean "from Rome".

"Roma have another name, a name more popular, but not correct. You know the Roma as Gypsies."

That Adora was a Gypsy was a bit of a surprise; her appearance did not fit the stereotype he had of that race of people. Still, David wasn't sure why being a Gypsy was a problem. Richard explained it patiently.

"The Roma are not always welcome in parts of Europe. For many years they have been hunted, chased from towns, their rights nonexistent."

David nodded. Somewhere back in school he had learned that. But then it was so far away, in time as well as place. "I guess I didn't realize such discrimination still existed."

"It does. And it doesn't. It depends on where you are."

"She doesn't even look like a gypsy...er...Roma." David's gaze had been drawn back to the window.

Richard laughed. "Not all Roma are dark and swarthy. It also depends on where they are from." He grew serious once more. "And who their parents are."

"And you? Are you a gyp...er, Roma...as well?"

For answer, Richard bowed an affirmative. He nodded toward the open window. "You have a beautiful wife."

David's smile turned fond. "Thank you. So do you."

"Your wife has a need to be tamed."

The air grew still and David wasn't sure he heard Richard right. "I beg your pardon?"

"I meant no insult to you, dear sir, only that her soul cries out to be tamed."

"As Adora is tamed."

Now it was Richard's turn to be nonplussed. "Adora? My sweet, adorable, beautiful Adora? Tamed?"

"Yes. She speaks not at all and seems quite docile. Isn't that the definition of tamed?

Now Richard grinned. "My dear sir, if you think Adora has been tamed, I regret to inform you, I am not man enough for that."

"I am totally confused by this conversation."

"Adora is a wonderful, independent spirit. She does some things I ask of her only because it suits her purpose. She is like a wild falcon that will sometimes come and sit on my arm because she loves me. But that is all. I could no more tame her than you can tame your wife."

"What makes you think I can't tame my wife?" David did not know whether he was being insulted or not.

"Because you love her too deeply."

The truth made David silent. Richard was right. Lissa wanted a stronger hand and he could not give it to her because he loved her too much to do so. David looked at his host as insight dawned.

"And you love Adora too much to tame her."

Richard nodded. "Now you understand."

* * * * *

Lissa eyed the shapely form of her hostess as the elegant woman scraped the dishes. The tiny kitchen had barely enough room for two people at the same time; how did one strike up a conversation with someone who never said a word? What if she were mute?

Lissa took the empty dinner plates from her and set them down on the counter, clearing her throat, somewhat out of unease, somewhat as a prelude to trying to say something. Adora chuckled.

It was the first noise Lissa had heard out of the woman. "Excuse me, did...did you just giggle?"

Adora grinned in response and turned on the water, filling the sink with soap bubbles.

Lissa shook her head, a lopsided grin of her own twisting her lips. "Sorry. It's just, well...we've met twice now and I've never heard even a single sound from you. I, um, I..." She didn't know how to proceed. Embarrassment colored her cheeks.

"It's all right," Adora said, her soft voice just carrying over the sound of the running water.

"I mean, if you're shy, I understand. I don't want to force you to talk to me if it makes you uncomfortable." In desperation, Lissa picked up a dishtowel and furiously dried the first dish Adora set in the drainer.

"I'm not shy. Nor could you force me to do anything I don't want to do." There was fierceness to the statement that stopped Lissa cold. The tone of Adora's voice belied the image of the silent icon Lissa had perceived her to be.

"I'm sorry, I didn't mean to offend you." Lissa finished drying the plate and reached for a second one, mentally vowing to keep her mouth shut lest her thoughtlessness get her into any further trouble.

"You didn't offend me." Adora's tone softened. "You really don't know what's going on here, do you?"

Lissa frowned. "I won't pretend I understand what kind of a relationship you have with...*Master* Richard." She spat the name out as if it left a bad taste in her mouth, even as her tongue wished to caress the words. "It's really none of my business."

Adora smiled but Lissa caught just a glimpse of pity in her eyes before the woman turned back to the dishes. "It will be your business before the evening is done. Mark my words."

"Why? How? Adora, I don't know what you're talking about."

"Don't you? I've seen the way you look at my husband."

Lissa stepped backward. How had Adora seen? She blinked several times as her mind ran back through the events of the evening. Had she slipped somehow? Let a glance linger a bit too long? When had her mask dropped? "I don't know what you're talking about."

"Oh?"

Adora's nonchalance was beginning to fray Lissa's nerves. "No, I don't. I know he's your husband, but I find him a bit overbearing, bossy, and...and..."

"Handsome?"

Lissa didn't answer.

"Sexy?"

Lissa turned her back on the woman.

"Alluring?"

Her nails dug into the back of the kitchen chair she clung to for support. Adora came up to her from behind, leaning in to whisper in her ear. "You want him to command you, even as you deny it."

Lissa shook her head. "No. No, I don't." Her voice was barely a whisper.

"You do. You want to be with him as much as your husband wants to be with me."

Lissa spun to face the woman. "You're seducing him. Just as...he...is trying to seduce me."

"Yes. You do understand."

"Why?"

"Because you both want to be seduced."

It was true. Lissa knew it. She did want Master Richard to seduce her, to talk her into his arms, just as she knew David would fall into Adora's arms if he knew Lissa wouldn't care. The damp dishtowel fell from her numb hands, unnoticed.

"Does it help you to know that Richard and I want the two of you as much as you want us?"

Lissa stared at the woman. "Why?"

"Because neither of us can give the other what is needed in the bedroom. Richard requires total and complete control, and so do I. We are both what are called 'dominants.' Do you know that word?"

Lissa nodded, and sank into the chair. "Pardon me, but I think I need to sit down. This is a bit much for me."

Adora nodded kindly, pulling out the chair beside her. With a gentle touch, she lifted Lissa's hand to hold in her own.

"I've handled this badly, I see that now. Perhaps I shouldn't have played the silent seductress role so long."

"It's an act?"

"Not really." Adora shrugged and tossed her blond tresses over her shoulder. "In meeting new people, I tend toward shyness, believe it or not. I have no talent whatsoever for small talk and tend to be much more forthright than society likes. So Richard and I play this game if we meet a couple we want to know better, he does the talking while I remain silent."

"And ensnare your victims."

Adora's laugh, genuine and hearty, melted a little of the ice wall Lissa had slammed up at the beginning of this conversation. Were she and David simply trophies, notches in the bedpost?

"When we went to dinner the other night, it was pure serendipitous chance that led us to your table. With a look, I let Richard know I wanted to play the game; your husband's reaction to me was most…pleasant."

"I'm sure it was. He was gawking like a teenage boy."

"The bulge in his pants certainly did not belong to a teenager. And I suspect you reaped the benefits of my work later that night?"

Lissa colored, remembering the best sex she'd had in years.

"I see I have hit the truth. Let me see if I can hit another one." Adora leaned forward and brushed a lock of hair from Lissa's face, putting her fingers under Lissa's chin and raising her face to look her in the eye. "You long for a man who can tame you. Inside you is a wild spirit that runs rampant over your heart. The man you married has captured your heart, but not this one part of your spirit. Am I right so far?"

The woman saw the truth; Lissa could only nod, not trusting her voice.

"But you are also afraid. It is not a part of you that can be wrenched away by force, but a part of you that you will freely give to the man who can conquer you. And that terrifies you. For if you find a man who can tame that wild mare inside, then you shall be fully taken. There will be no part of you unclaimed by a man. Your entire being will belong to others."

Even as she heard the words spoken, Lissa's heart leapt and her body became aroused. This was exactly her desire — and her fear. Numb, she nodded again, unshed tears forming in her eyes.

"I may have Roma blood that flows in my veins, but I cannot foretell the future. No one really can." Adora let go of Lissa's hands and pulled away, breaking the moment. "If Richard is that man, I don't know. But I know you want to find out."

* * * * *

The four of them met again in the exotic living room, but no one made a move to sit down. Richard and Adora had given David and Lissa much to think about and to discuss. David found himself eyeing his hostess in a new light; Richard had explained her dominance, and the fact that he suspected it wasn't real. She only lacked the right man to bring out her submissive nature. Was he that man? Or would she eat him alive as she had others, by Richard's telling?

Lissa's glances from under her lashes were speculative as well. Did she have the courage to let this giant Roma king see the "wild mare" Adora alluded to? She would not be the first submissive he had taken on; Adora had told her there had been a few others, some successful, some not. From what Adora didn't say, Lissa knew her hostess was one of the failures, no matter how much they loved each other.

The leave taking was swift as there was little left to talk about. Small talk had somehow become just that— small. Taking their leave, David and Lissa walked the short distance to the car, got in, and drove home in silence.

After a few years of marriage, partners know when the other needs time to think, and both David and Lissa recognized that in the other. While David speculated about what Adora told Lissa behind that swinging door, Lissa wondered if Master Richard told David he wanted to subjugate Lissa. Occupied so much with their private thoughts, the two arrived at home, prepared for bed and slid under the covers. In the darkness, the pillow talk brought out their concerns.

Lissa began. "You know Adora's trying to seduce you."

David countered. "And Richard intends to seduce you."

The two lay on their backs, staring up at the ceiling, only the sides of their bodies touching. Lissa took a deep breath and plunged in. "I guess then, the question is, 'Do we want to let them?'"

"What would it mean to us, if we did? I love you, Lissa, and I don't want to lose you." He rolled to his side and faced his wife, but still did not reach out to her.

"I love you, too, David. You are the man I want to spend the rest of my life with." She too, rolled to face him, her hand on his cheek. Muted light from the street lamps outside gave her enough light to see his face, but not read it.

"He thinks he can tame you."

She grinned. "Oh, he does, does he? He just might find out I'm not such a pushover as he thinks I am!"

"But you want that, don't you? You want to find someone who can push you into that submissiveness."

"Yes." For the first time in a long time, she was totally honest with her husband. Tonight there could be nothing less than that.

"And I love you too much to take you that way. I just can't do it, Lissa."

"I know that, David." Her heart went out to her husband. He had tried. He really had. But it just wasn't him. She snuggled closer and nuzzled her nose under his chin, getting comfortable in his arms. "It's all right. You tried. That means a lot to me."

"But it would mean more if I allowed that side of you to express itself in the manner it needs expressing." He cuddled his wife the way he so enjoyed; her skin soft under his hands.

She pulled away a bit to try and fathom what was in his eyes, but it was too dark. "What do you mean?"

"I mean, if you want to be with Richard for sex, I think it would be all right with me."

There it was. Permission granted. But she knew the catch; she had to agree that he could "play" with Adora. Still David's phrasing gave her pause. "You think? Sounds as if you're still not sure."

"I'm not. I want you to be happy, Lissa. And I know this one part of our marriage is not happy. For either of us."

"So you want me to give you permission to fuck Adora."

"Lissa!"

She giggled. Using such language was not something she usually did. Although she had to admit, the somewhat dirty word turned her on. As did the thought of sharing her husband.

"I want you to be happy as well, David. And I think you might find Adora a bit, well, a bit of a challenge. She's not the meek and mild woman I think you're expecting to find."

"I know that."

"How? She hasn't said a word to you!"

"Richard told me he cannot tame her because he loves her too much, that she has a very independent spirit. And her eyes speak volumes, even when her voice says nothing."

"She's a dominant, David. Do you know what that means?"

David laughed. "Yes, my dear heart, I do. I've been trying to be one for you, remember?"

Lissa sat up on one arm. "David, are you telling me you are submissive?" She wasn't sure how she felt about that. David was her equal in all things, but she wasn't sure she wanted him equal in this. Somehow she needed him to be stronger than her in *something*.

"No, I am not submissive. I've also read about that. I know this is hard for you to understand, but I think I am dominant…just not with you."

Understanding came. "You think you can tame Adora, but not me, just as Master Richard can't tame her, but thinks he can tame me."

David laughed. "We'll leave your sentence structure aside for a bit, teacher." He bussed her nose with his lips. "But yes, you have it right." He rolled onto his back again, gathering his thoughts. "Richard seems to think Adora also has a need to be tamed, just as you do. But that he's not the one to do it because he loves her too much."

"Just like you love me too much?" It was beginning to all make sense to Lissa.

"Yes."

"So you want to swap wives for sex."

It sounded so…naughty. So perverse. So arousing and sexy.

"Yes."

Lissa let the word hang in the silence for a moment, then, with her heart beating hard and feigning a nonchalant attitude, she lay down beside her husband as well, her face to the ceiling. "I can live with that."

It was David's turn to sit up, rolling onto one arm as he tried to read his wife's face in the dim light. "Really? Lissa, do you mean that?"

She grinned. While her heart still beat wildly, she knew her answer. "Yes, David. I do mean that. If you and Richard want to arrange it, I will go along with it."

Immediately the image of her bound body, naked before Richard's gaze popped into her head and she felt her arousal spread between her legs. "Do you think ill of me, because I want you to share me with another man?"

For answer, David simply took Lissa's hand and put it on his rock-hard cock. She laughed as she closed her warm fingers around him, loving the feel of that rigid stiffness. "When you say it like that, 'sharing you with another man,' this happens," David whispered into her ear.

"And I tingle at the thought of being shared." She guided his hand to her warm and very wet pussy. He dipped his fingers deep before bringing them up to rub them on her nipples, spreading her juices to cover them in turn. The little buds turned as hard as David's cock, swelling under his touch.

"I see the thought turns you on as well," David murmured into her ear.

Lissa didn't want him to stop; her husband's hands roamed across her skin, setting it on fire as thoughts of Richard's domination once again flitted through her imagination. With one difference: this time, there was a very real possibility of those fantasies becoming reality. She whimpered in the back of her throat at the thought and moved her hips closer to David's cock. "Take me."

David needed no other urging. His wife's obvious arousal at the turn this conversation had taken urged him on. "And Adora? How does it make you feel that I'd be with another woman?"

Relieved. But she didn't say it. Never could she go off with another man if David hadn't given her permission. And never if she knew her husband was, in any way, being slighted. But to know he would be as satisfied as she was? She moaned out loud and pushed herself at him again. "Now, David. Please...take me."

He liked it when she begged, although he hadn't been sure it was fitting between a husband and wife. Tonight, he didn't care. His cock throbbed with life and desire; he wanted nothing more than to sink it into Lissa's pussy as he imagined himself thrusting into Adora.

As a result, he was rougher than usual. Throwing Lissa's leg out of his way, he knelt before her open pussy and grabbed his wife's thighs. With a strong pull, he yanked her toward him, pausing only a moment to change his grip on her before impaling her with his cock.

Lissa yelped at the sudden thrust, but did not protest. She couldn't. Raising her arms to grab the wrought iron headboard, she imagined herself tied and used by Master Richard as David repeatedly thrust his cock into her. She knew from his expression, that he imagined her to be Adora, and that was fine by her. His roughness excited her; the blood pounded in her ears in time to David's thrusts. She felt her pussy lips swell with need; her moans filled the room.

David's grunts grew louder and his thrusts faster. And when Lissa screamed and her pussy contracted around his cock, the world inside his head exploded and his seed burst forth to fill her quivering body.

Spent, he collapsed beside her, for once not immediately handing her tissues to clean up with. Lissa didn't reach for them either. Instead, she pulled herself up to snuggle in his arms, exhausted by the emotions of the night.

"There are still many questions to be answered." David's voice, barely a whisper, sounded in her ear.

"In the morning," was all Lissa could answer before she drifted off to sleep.

Chapter 3

But the morning afforded David and Lissa no time for conversation. The alarm went off and immediately the two scrambled into the normal early-morning rush off to work. A peck on the lips and a fast farewell and the two parted ways until dinner.

Lissa prided herself on her professionalism, so thoughts of last night's lovemaking and the events that precipitated it remained in the back of her mind all day. Only on the ride home did she have the luxury of bringing them forward and examining the possibilities—and the dangers.

By the time she reached home, Lissa convinced herself all this was a bad idea. What did they really know about this couple? Who knew what kind of diseases they might have? What if they were really slavers and wanted to sell her into servitude?

Okay, the last one was a little farfetched and Lissa giggled as she pulled into the drive of their modest city home. Since David wasn't home yet, she followed her normal custom, going upstairs to change into comfortable shorts and a tank top before starting dinner.

* * * * *

David Patterson was not one to rush into anything. Ever. So the fact that he and Lissa had even gotten to the discussion stage of swapping partners after meeting this couple only twice still amazed him. Were things moving too fast? In the cold light of day, it seemed he and Lissa were headed for trouble.

But what exciting trouble it could be if only Lissa would go along. That was the sticking point. Richard had made it very clear last night that they were a package deal. David could not have Adora unless Richard got Lissa.

And did he mind if Lissa went off with another man? Could he trust Richard not to harm his wife? Questions crowded his mind as he entered the house.

"Lissa? I'm home." Plopping his briefcase down on a dining room chair, he headed into the kitchen.

"Here!" Lissa's voice, however, came from upstairs, not her usual spot. David followed her voice and found her in the bedroom, sitting cross-legged on the edge of the bed and holding her Velcro cuffs in her hands. The evening sun caught the rich auburn highlights of her hair where it cascaded across her bare shoulders, the pink tank top straps almost hidden by the dark curls. Her slender legs folded under, spring-white since the summer was still young and neither of them had yet had much time in the sun. Lissa turned the cuffs over and over in her hands as if weighing one against the other. Or as if she were trying to decide which was better.

"What are you doing?"

She didn't look up from the cuffs. "Thinking about what I really want."

David's heart lurched for her; it was obvious she was torn and he was pushing her too fast. He sat beside her on the bed, prepared for her answer. This was it. She was about to tell him to stuff it.

"What have you decided?" David's gentle voice belied the tension he felt inside.

"Not much," Lissa admitted. "David, there are two constants at work here, and what I can't tell is if they're mutually compatible or mutually exclusive."

"Okay, I'll bite. What are the two constants?" David tried not to show his relief that she did not dismiss the idea out of hand.

"The first one, and the most important one, is that I love you."

She looked at him, her eyes so open and honest that it almost hurt. David reached out to cup her cheek with his hand; the depth of her emotion took away all his doubts about losing her.

"I love you, Lissa Marie Patterson. You are right. That is a constant. The only way our love can grow is deeper."

His tender smile brought tears to her eyes. She closed them as he bent toward her, leaning into their gentle kiss. His scent intoxicated her as it always did. The loving touch of his lips did nothing to ease her guilt over her desires.

And when they moved apart, and she remained silent, David prompted her to say what was still unsaid. "And the second constant?"

"These." Lissa held up the cuffs as her shoulders sagged in defeat. "I keep trying to tell myself that this is just a silly schoolgirl fantasy — to want to be tied up and 'forced' to do things. Sexual things." She shook her head. Not even to David could she divulge her wildest desires. "I keep trying to tell myself to snap out of it." Lissa swallowed hard, took a deep breath, and blurted out the second constant. "But the reality is that I don't want to snap out of it. I want to live it. Completely. I want to be 'owned' as a sex slave."

The words sounded ludicrous to her ears, but David did not laugh. He sighed. "I know." Taking one of the cuffs, he played with it; putting together, then ripping apart the Velcro fastenings. "And since I can't give you that personally, I want to give you to a man who can."

Lissa shivered even as David's words aroused her. "You speak as if I'm a piece of property you can just dispense with any way you see fit."

"Aren't you? Isn't that a part of what you want?"

Lissa hesitated. Wasn't it? "Yes, but what about—"

"No, 'yes, buts.' Is it, or isn't it?"

The sternness in David's voice took her by surprise and brought out her defiant side. "Yes, then. Yes, I want to be given to a man who can handle me."

David grinned, but there was little mirth in his eyes. "And what happens if he tames you? Takes you and claims you as his own?"

Lissa understood his concern; it was hers as well. What if David decided he liked Adora more than he liked her? She could only answer from her own heart and simply. "Because of the first constant, that can't happen. I love you."

David heard the words, but saw in her eyes a faint flicker of doubt. Did she doubt herself? Or him?

"And I love you, Lissa. I always will."

"Even when you're with Adora?"

"Yes, even when I'm with Adora. She will satisfy certain hungers inside me, I think. But she could never take your place. Just as I hope Richard never takes mine. No matter how much of a compliant slave you become for him."

Lissa smiled at the thought being tamed. No matter how much her soul might cry out for it, her logical and rational mind would fight her; this Lissa knew. It would be a long time before she would do anything a man commanded her to do just because he commanded it.

David's stomach growled, breaking the somber mood. "Come on, dinner's on me tonight."

"As long as we don't go to the diner. I don't think I'm ready for another night like the last time we were there!"

* * * * *

"So what do you think?"

David and Lissa ended up at a large Chinese buffet for dinner. The crowd was noisy, and a child ran past their table with his plate filled with pastries instead of main dishes. It was as unsexy a place as one could find and Lissa thought it just the right spot to continue their conversation. A place where cold, rational thought could hold sway. No danger of the two of them getting so hot at the ideas that they ended up having sex again and not finishing the conversation. Although last night certainly had been…interesting.

"David, what do you think?" Lissa tapped her fork on David's plate to get his attention.

"About?"

"About swapping partners!" Lissa hissed the words in a low voice; the noise of the restaurant would only cover so much.

"I'm leaning toward it."

"What's holding you back?"

"What's pushing you forward? I thought you were the one with all the reservations before."

"I still have them. I just want to know what your concerns are. I already know mine."

"My biggest concern is for your safety, Lissa. You'll be in a position where you can't get loose if you decide you want out of there. I know, I know!" David held up his chopsticks as she started to protest. "You'll use a safeword. But I have only his word of honor that he will use it; that if you call it out, he'll stop."

Lissa kept her eyes on her plate so David would not see them twinkle with mischief. How could she explain to him the power of that very thought? The helplessness, the inability to stop the man from having his way, was exactly what moved her, swayed her primal spirit. She tried to put it into words. "That's a part of what makes it so arousing. Not knowing if he'll stop when I ask him to, or ignore my pleadings and keep on going."

"You're not making me feel any better about that angle."

She shook her head. "I'm sorry. I guess I just can't explain it very well. Do you trust Master Richard?"

David nodded as he toyed with his food. "I do. But I'm not sure if my trust is clouded by…other desires."

Lissa giggled at his circumvented reference. "Which is why I need a chance to meet him myself. Without you in the room. I want to make my own decision."

"I can understand that. I'd like the opportunity to talk to Adora as well, privately. It's important to me to know she's not being coerced into anything."

"Same here. Although I think I say with some certainty that she's as independent as I am." Lissa remembered the gypsy woman's hands in hers as they spoke the night before. How naïve Lissa had felt in her presence. David was in for a bit of a surprise, she thought.

"So is that the only thing holding you back? My safety?"

"No, there is one other thing."

Lissa knew its importance by the way he deliberately set down his chopsticks across the top of his plate. "I know you love me, Lissa, and I love you. But a part of my heart is terrified you'll want him over me."

"And a part of me is terrified you'll want Adora over me. But that's not going to happen, David. I love you. Not him. I want him only for what he can do for me sexually. This is pure lust. Nothing more. I'm not going to glorify what I want to do with any fancy words. I want Richard to tie me up and fuck my brains out. That's it. Then I want to come home to my life and my house...and my husband."

Her voice got a little louder than she intended and the older couple in the booth across the way from them gave them several frowns before turning back to their own dinners.

"Well, that's all I want from Adora, too." David leaned forward, keeping his voice low and throwing a few glances back at the older couple. "Just sex." He grinned. "Well, at least our motivations are not complicated!"

Lissa giggled, feeling as if a weight had dropped from her shoulders. The two of them wanted the same things; she wasn't pushing David into something he didn't want.

"So what do we do next? How do we arrange it so that you can have some private time to talk to Adora and I can talk to Richard all by himself?" The thought of being alone with him gave her goosebumps.

"Let me call Richard when we get home and talk it over with him. Will you let us take care of the details? Or do you want to be a part of the conversation?"

Lissa shook her head and then grinned. "No, I think I like the fact that my husband is arraigning to 'give me away' for a night. You go ahead and handle all the grunt work. Just tell me what to wear and what time to show up!"

David snorted his soft drink. "Wish you were always this compliant."

She laughed. "No, you don't. Too many decisions you'd have to make on your own. Like whether to plant red flowers out front or white." This was one of their running gags. Each year Lissa would ask David what color he'd like out front and each year David's answer was the same. "Color. Put some color out front. You decide what plants and what colors. Just color."

"Okay, point conceded. We owe them a dinner, so perhaps that's what we'll do. Have them over for dinner and afterward, I'll take Adora off, and you spend some time with Richard. If everything clicks, well, we'll take care of that if and when it happens."

* * * * *

David informed her later that everything was arranged; Richard and Adora were coming for dinner Saturday night. That way neither of them would have to rush home from work to prepare dinner.

The rest of the week flew by. Every night David would put his arms around Lissa in bed, cuddling her, making sure she understood how much he loved her. And every night Lissa would snuggle into his warmth, grateful and loving, and nervous.

Saturday each of them took their time getting ready, both wanting to look good, but both concerned that the other might get jealous. David came into the bath and caught Lissa wiping off her makeup for the second time.

"What was wrong with the way you looked?"

"Oh, David!" Lissa threw her hands down in exasperation. "If I put on too much makeup you'll think I'm getting all gussied up for him. If I don't put on any makeup, *he'll* think I don't care about my appearance!" She glared at him in the mirror. "I can't win!"

David laughed. "I love that you're afraid to make me jealous." His hands encircled her waist and he leaned forward to give her a peck on the cheek. "Don't worry. I want you to be as drop-dead gorgeous as you always are."

She batted playfully at the top of his head. "Out, liar. Let me get this makeup on."

He couldn't resist a playful swat on her rear end as he left, gratified by the surprise in her eyes. At least he didn't need to worry about all that stuff. Lissa didn't wear makeup at all on a daily basis and David actually preferred her real face. But he understood her need to look "better" tonight.

Khaki pants and a light shirt was all he needed to look good. He finished buttoning the shirt and examined his appearance in Lissa's full-length mirror. With his fingers, he brushed his straight sandy hair off his forehead, making a mental note that he needed a haircut. As it was, it touched the tops of his ears; he could almost tuck it behind. A stray lock kept falling down over his eyes; maybe Adora would find it sexy. It gave him a bit of a rakish look and he raised an eyebrow seductively at his reflection. A cocky rogue stared back at him and David laughed.

"Nope. Just me tonight, Adora, honey. No tricks, no pretenses. Let's just see what happens."

"Who are you talking to?"

David grinned at Lissa's towel-clad body. "Just myself. Although I could try my wiles on you, baby!" He raised his suggestive eyebrow and wiggled it at her.

Lissa laughed. "Not me, sonny-boy! I have other toys to play with tonight. Now out so I can dress in peace." She scooted him out the door.

She had chosen her clothes carefully for the evening— a V-necked blouse that showed a bit, but not too much. A light muslin skirt that hid as much as it revealed, and simple, low-heeled sandals. Several times she had to remind herself that nothing would happen tonight. Conversation only. She would sound out Master Richard's philosophies regarding bondage, Dominance, and submission. And did she have the nerve to bring up S&M? How many times had she imagined that flogger? No. Best to leave that hidden for a while yet. Stick with safe topics. What kind of Dom was he? What did he expect of her? And more importantly, did his vision of a D/s relationship match her own?

A car pulled into the drive and Lissa started. Her mind had gone off again, once more envisioning Richard's strong hands closing over her breasts. With one last pull of the comb through her hair, she hurried downstairs to greet her guests.

* * * * *

Richard dressed in his customary color, black shoes, black pants, and black, partly unbuttoned shirt. All of it designed to set off his swarthy skin and mane of curly black hair, presenting a romantic look of power and authority.

Lissa's visceral response to his appearance and authority made her stomach flip as she studied the dark goatee that circled those incredible lips. Damn, but the man was gorgeous! As Richard stepped into the house, Lissa tried not to stare at the mat of curly, black hair that peeked through his open collar. What would it be like to run her fingers through? But when their eyes met, she forgot his chest.

Latent power emanated from those sea-blue, gypsy king eyes; power that entranced, mesmerized. With difficulty, Lissa tore her eyes away when Adora entered behind him. Giving the woman a hug gave Lissa a chance to recover.

What was there about seeing two women exchange even an innocent hug that excited him so? David's own eyes twinkled as Lissa and Adora greeted one another; for a brief moment, he envisioned them both on their knees before him. He exchanged glances with Richard and knew the other man had the same thought.

"A bottle of wine for our hosts." Richard handed David a bottle of Rkatsiteli.

"I don't know this wine," David stumbled over the pronunciation.

"It comes from the Ukraine. Not easy to get here in this country. I found only one vineyard that grows it, Dr. Konstantin Frank's in New York State. Incredible to have found it at all."

"Thank you. Shall we have it now?"

"It is better as an after-dinner drink. It tends to be sweeter than the more available American wines."

Lissa listened to the exchange, mentally shaking her head. Why wasn't she surprised that Master Richard also knew about wines? But she remained silent and led the way into the living room. They were having pasta tonight and the water wasn't quite ready. She would remain with their guests as she waited for the water to boil.

David directed Richard to the big easy chair, Adora took the stool by his side; David and Lissa shared the couch. As before, Adora said nothing, although either Lissa was getting better at reading the woman's smiles, or Adora was hiding her meaning less; there was an impish quality to the goddess' smiles this night and every one of them was meant for David.

He was not immune to them. Each time Adora smiled, the room grew warmer; soon it would be impossible to hide the growing bulge in his pants. The thought of someday having that woman's lips around his cock...

Lissa stood, needing to check on dinner; very aware that Richard's eyes were upon her every move. A small part of her wanted to be annoyed at his attentions; the man surveyed her as if she were on display. But another part of her was feeling naughty, so she waggled her hips a little as she took her wantonness into the kitchen to hide. Her courage only took her so far.

The dinner conversation remained neutral, the strong sexual tension playing counterpoint to the men's discussions of world events. David sat at the head of the small, rectangular dining room table; Lissa sat to his right. Richard sat in the secondary place of honor opposite David; Adora smiled at Lissa across the table. Although his words were directed at her husband, Richard's dark eyes constantly engaged Lissa's. When she passed him the basket of rolls and their hands touched, she couldn't help but let her hand linger a moment longer than she should have. While the man said nothing, his eyes searched into her soul until Lissa looked down and away, pulling her hands back to fiddle self-consciously with her napkin. The slight pressure from David's knee on hers gave her reassurance that they were in this together.

As the dinner wound down, the conversation shifted. David opened and poured the white wine Richard brought; Lissa sipped it with caution. The pleasant taste lingered on her palate; obviously Master Richard had excellent taste in wines. The four of them remained in their seats, casually sipping the sweet, exotic wine and Richard mentioned he and Adora had been together for fifteen years; he smiled at his wife as he spoke and extended his hand, palm up toward her. The indulgent grin she gave him as she slipped her slender hand into his belied her quiet nature; Lissa glimpsed the untamed tiger that hid inside the woman. Did David see it as well?

If he did, David gave no indication. "Lissa and I have been married for seven years; long enough to know we are not compatible in all ways."

And there it was. Out in the open for discussion. The elephant in the room had been given an introduction. Lissa glanced nervously at her guests, but their smiles had only deepened. Was she the only one with qualms?

Richard squeezed Adora's hand and swirled the wine in his glass. "There is something to be said for having the courage to acknowledge your different needs." Lissa watched from under her eyelashes as the commanding bearing of the Gypsy king emerged once more, his wine catching the candlelight and tossing it around the glass like little stars. "My Adora and I, too, have different tastes in one particular area of our lives." His eyes looked meaningfully over the rim of the glass and straight at Lissa. No mirth emanated from those dark eyes, only raw power and lust.

"Lissa." David's strong tone caught her ear and she tore her eyes away from the challenge in Richard's eyes, trying to focus on her husband on her right.

"Yes, David?" She gave herself a mental shake to refocus her thoughts on the fact that there were other people in the room.

"I would like you to accompany Richard outside; show him the deck while Adora and I clear the table." Dealing with the dishes would give his hands something to do as he spoke with the goddess. When the blond turned and smiled at him, rising gracefully from the table, David calmed the sudden butterflies that rose in his stomach. Could he really tame her? Or would she end up taming him?

So intent on his own nervousness, he did not notice the exasperated look Lissa shot him as she, too, rose with grace and gestured Richard out through the French doors to the deck at the back of the house.

David knew it wasn't exactly hospitable to make a guest clear the dishes, but he needed to give Lissa and Richard a chance to talk, just as he needed time to talk to Adora. Except that once in the kitchen with all the dishes, he wasn't sure how to begin. Using the scraping of dishes to cover his momentary loss, he simply smiled at her when she brought over a dish to be scraped. But there was no mistaking the "come-hither" smile she gave him in return. Or the way she pressed her leg to his as he stood before the sink.

Her blue eyes shone in the kitchen light. Not the same blue as his own, however, more the blue of a cornflower on a hot summer afternoon that complimented the faint blush of her cheek; the blush of pale peaches against the cream of her skin. Words were unnecessary. He leaned toward her and she met his lips with hers; full, luscious lips, ripe lips that tasted faintly of the strange, sweet wine. Her perfume filled his senses; the scent of a garden just coming to blossom.

And when they parted, David glimpsed just how to "tame the wildcat" Richard and Lissa had seen inside this woman. It wasn't really taming she needed, but refuge. "Fiercely independent" Richard had called her before. That she was—any fool could see that. But David suspected a softer side; one that wanted somewhere warm and safe and comfortable. Her forwardness was just an act. He was sure of it.

He took the woman's hands, turning them over, examining the long slender fingers, one pinky slightly bent as if it had once been broken. Gently, he raised the bent finger to his lips, kissing away the hurt. Her look of surprise touched his compassionate heart.

David led her through the small passage that connected the kitchen to the front foyer, then into the living room. Sitting her down on the couch, he kept his distance, while still holding her hand. Lissa would have recognized the look on David's face at that moment: it was one she had seen often. She privately called it his "angel face." Patience, understanding, wisdom from more than one lifetime all seemed to be wrapped up in his eyes. "Tell me?"

Adora could not resist. She saw the acceptance in his eyes. Unlike other men, she could tell him anything and he would not judge her. Could he, however, handle the whole truth? Here in his American house? Living his sheltered, American life? In the past, she shocked her lovers, dominating them with her story. This time she simply wanted to find peace.

Her voice halted at first, then grew in strength. "Here in America, your media praises women with blond hair and blue eyes. That was not so in the small town where I grew up. Or perhaps I should make that plural—the small *towns*. They tend to all get mixed up in my mind. There were so many of them. We would move into a small place, all five of us: my grandparents, my uncle, my mother and me. I didn't know my father; my mother never spoke of him. It wasn't until much later that I finally figured that part out."

Bitterness crept into her voice, but David did not interrupt. Let her get the whole thing out. Only then could they deal with the pain she carried.

"My hair made it impossible for me to hide. Even when I was very little, people used to point at me and whisper things I didn't understand. And then when I got older, the other children would make fun of me. Often the girls tried to pick fights with me. By then I knew it wasn't just my appearance that set me apart, but the fact that we were Roma."

She looked at David, expecting the same blank look she got whenever she told people that. Lissa had had that look the other night. But David didn't. Since his conversation with Richard the other night, he had been online trying to find out as much as he could about the plight of Gypsies in their native lands. What he had learned had shocked and disturbed him. "Gypsy" was a term given the nomadic people by Europeans who thought they originated in Egypt. They hadn't. The people preferred to be called the Roma, and near as he could figure out, much of their heritage came from India. Strict rules governed the Roma; rules Master Richard and Adora did not follow. Still, it was not in him to judge another person by rules he didn't fully understand. The Roma were a persecuted people. Did Adora have first-hand knowledge of that persecution?

"Adora, I won't pretend to understand why people behave so stupidly. It happens here, too. Only with us, it's by race—black and white. Why your people are so persecuted makes as much sense to me as judging someone by their skin color. Which is to say, no sense at all." When she did not immediately continue, David squeezed her hand, trying to reassure her.

Realizing that David knew more than she had given him credit for, Adora hesitated. The last thing she wanted or needed was pity. One trace of that in his manner and her walls would slam up letting the dominatrix take over. But his words made sense to her. She hadn't thought of America's troubles with race as a parallel to her own experiences with prejudice, but he was right. The details might differ, but intolerance was the same no matter what guise it wore. Perhaps he did understand.

"When I was fifteen, we moved again. By that time, my uncle was the only one supporting us; my grandfather had grown too old. My mother would sew in the shops when they would hire her, but her eyes were going bad — most of those places didn't have good light.

"This time when we moved I refused to go back to school. There wasn't much in the way of education going on anyway. Mostly it was a place for the local bullies to gather. Instead, I looked for a job, finding one with a fairly prominent family. They needed someone to watch their children for a few hours each day.

"It wasn't difficult work, and I soon discovered little children don't yet have their parent's attitudes. They greeted me each day with open arms, accepting me for who I was. I did not try to hide the nomadic life my family led, having been chased from more than one town. But the mother didn't seem to mind.

"I worked there for three months. It was bliss. She paid me well; I never saw the husband as he was working out of town. The children loved me; I loved them. The first people other than my family I came to trust."

She fell silent again and David's heart sank. He suspected this story did not have a happy ending.

"One day I arrived at my normal hour, but the house was empty. I called, wondering where they were. Everything seemed fine; the children's toys were scattered as normal. I went upstairs to be sure they knew I was there, just in case the children were sleeping, but no one was home. I was on my way down the stairs again when I saw him.

"I had met the father only once before, the day I was hired. Why he was home this day, I never found out. I reminded him that I was the children's nanny and that it was my usual time to work. He informed me that his wife had taken the children on holiday and that my services were not needed for the next several days. The casual relationship I had with his wife made me forget my place. To be without the money I made would mean difficulties for my family. He told me there were other ways I could earn the money.

"Life as Roma means nothing to most people. But we have our pride and I knew what he meant by the look in his eye. I told him no, I'd find work elsewhere."

Her eyes narrowed, growing hard as she remembered that far-off time as if it were still before her. She would tell him all and he would understand why she was dominant and why he would bow before her. "He did not take my 'no' for an answer, David. He dragged me into the children's room and raped me on the floor. And when he was done, he tied me to the crib and called in his friends."

David wanted to put his arms around her; to hold her and tell her it was all right. But there was defiance in her eyes; he remained still. Her hand gripped his as she controlled her fierce anger and bitterness. "I want to know it all," he growled as an anger of his own began to grow.

"There were four of them. Not one part of me was left undamaged. They shoved their cocks into my virgin holes and thrust their way to their own satisfaction. And when they were done, they left me tied, bleeding and crying, to the baby's crib. They profaned the most sacred place in the world to me.

"I have no idea how many times that night they took me. Either time has erased much of the rest of that night, or I have removed it from my memory. My mother later found me collapsed outside our own house. We knew better than to go to the authorities. Instead we moved. And moved again when I was stopped one afternoon by boys who wanted the same thing. Their assault was interrupted, or I think I would not be alive today."

A calm, matter-of-factness colored her voice now as the strong-willed woman finished her story. With a level gaze, she watched David struggle with the information she so brutally shared.

"You have told Richard all this."

She nodded. "I met Richard after my grandparents died and my uncle finally fled. I don't blame him. Family is important to the Roma, but how could he hope to find happiness and a wife of his own when tied to his sister and niece? I was glad he escaped our poverty.

"My mother grew ill; I took her to a local hospital. But we had no money to pay the nurses or doctors and they would not look at her. I pleaded with them. That's when Master Richard came to my aid. He bullied the nurse on duty into calling the doctor to look at my mother. But we had come too late, they said. She had advanced pneumonia. That night, she died in my arms in a hospital bed he paid for.

"By then I was eighteen. Old enough to accept the ways of the world. I offered myself to him in order to pay for the bills my mother's death produced. He accepted."

"He accepted? That's slavery!"

"That's business, David."

"To demand you give him sex for paying your bills is a business that has a name in this country!" David's anger grew again; and the target was just outside his house, talking with his wife.

Adora laughed for the first time since she began her story. "No, David, not like that."

"What? I don't understand. You said you offered yourself and he accepted."

"He did. But he did not want me sexually. He told me he needed someone to help him in his work. Someone he could train in his methods. I would live in his home and help him. For the first time in my life I had a room of my own."

Chastened, David nodded.

"When did you fall in love with him?"

"Long after he fell in love with me. He told me, years later, that he'd fallen in love with me the moment he saw me in the hospital, fighting with the nurse in order to get someone to examine my mother. We'd been together for almost three years before I looked at him one day and realized I loved him."

"Just like that?"

"Just like that."

It was clear to David that Adora had not told him the whole story. From the little he had read of the Roma culture, much of what she said about the ostracism made sense. But other parts didn't quite fit. But he could be patient. He still had a great deal to learn on his own.

* * * * *

Lissa sipped the Rkatsiteli to cover the awkward silence stretching between them. She savored the rich, sweet taste of the exotic wine as she thought of and discarded several conversation starters. Master Richard leaned against the rail of the deck; light from the dining room spilled out through the sheer curtains giving his features an erotic, romantic cast. How did one begin a conversation with a man she was considering giving her total submission to?

Richard said nothing, only patting the railing beside him. With trepidation, Lissa obeyed his silent invitation, moving forward to stand next to him in the dim light. Was this what submissives did?

The woman's very uncertainty intrigued him. The husband had been easy to read; he wore his desires on his face and in his eyes. But the woman before him guarded her secrets, secrets he knew how to unlock.

"You are a very beautiful woman, Melissa."

Her formal name. Somehow it sounded sexy when he said it. His baritone voice; soft, intense, powerful, seductive, pulled her body, and she took a half-step nearer.

"You love your husband and yet you yearn for a different embrace."

Her whisper on the warm night air barely breathed her desire. "Yes."

"Tell me, Melissa Patterson, what is it you want above all else?"

His eyes sank into her soul, plumbing the depths of her yearnings; she let him plunge. Power emanated from every cell of his Roma blood; her desires were stripped away, one by one, until the core of her being stood naked before his gaze. He knew what she wanted even as she could not admit her conflicted desires; his power penetrated her defenses. Her mouth opened, but she could only shake her head.

"You are silent because you do not truly know what it is you need. You are afraid to face the darkest parts of your desire." Richard's fingers traced the line of her cheekbone and Lissa turned her face into his hand, ashamed and afraid even as she sought comfort.

"You have read of sexual slavery?"

Lissa's breath caught and she nodded.

"But you do not know where the line is between the submissiveness you wish to give and the slavery your heart fears."

Lissa pulled away, making an attempt at reassembling her wits. Turning away from him, she took several deep breaths and managed to put some semblance of her guard back in place. Online, she had read of Master/slave relationships; many had rules the slave was expected to follow and punishments for even the smallest infraction. That wasn't what she was looking for—at all. Her voice was strong when she turned to answer him. "I am not a slave."

"No, you are not."

"And I don't think I want to be one."

"It is too early to tell if you could manage it. There are many steps for you to explore first. Such a decision would be a long way off yet."

Richard did not move from his position, casually leaning against the railing, making an occasional gesture with his wineglass. Where Lissa fidgeted and paced over the small deck, he remained still, a constant while the storm whirled around him.

"I do like bondage." Lissa turned away from him, making her admission to the backyard.

"Yes."

"And I don't want choices. I don't want someone constantly saying, 'How are you doing?' That drives me nuts. I know you need to check, but you'll need to find a different way to say it." She didn't even notice the pronoun change. No longer did she address a mythical Master, but the one who stood beside her.

"Because you don't want me to really care how you are doing."

"Exactly! I mean, I want you to care, but I don't want to know that you care." She stamped her foot in frustration. "This isn't making any sense."

"Sit down, woman."

Lissa's tempest paused. Richard had not moved, yet there was a subtle difference in his manner. An order had been given. Swallowing hard, Lissa did as she was told.

Still Richard did not move from his spot at the rail. He sipped from his glass before taking on a more pedantic tone. Time to make her stop wavering and climb down off the fence.

"You want a man you can trust."

He paused as she considered the outwardly simple statement. Of course she wanted someone she could trust. She wasn't going to let just anybody tie her up and fuck her. What was he thinking?

"You want a man you can trust."

Richard stood, setting his glass on the rail. His voice was softer this time, more intent. She nodded, her eyes narrowing. What was he getting at?

"You want a man you can trust."

With slow steps, he moved toward her, keeping her gaze locked in his eyes as he sat beside her at the small table.

"You want to abandon yourself, completely and thoroughly. You do not want to have to think. You want to let someone else make the decisions, let him handle all your concerns. You want simply to exist for one purpose — to fulfill his sexual needs and in doing so, have him fulfill your own. You want to be free to experience wild orgasms, free to give a man total pleasure. You want a man you can trust."

He spoke her truest desires. She could only nod, her eyes filling with tears of longing. He put into words the confusion of her soul.

"The question becomes, can you trust me?" He stood, purposefully breaking the moment. He returned to his position at the rail, picking up his glass once more as he turned from her and watched the faint stars over the backyard.

Lissa blinked back her tears and cleared her throat. After a moment, she rose, smoothing her skirt out of habit. Her wineglass still sat on the rail where she had set it earlier. Holding her chin high, she strode over to him and picked it up.

"I don't know if I trust you yet, Master Richard. I will admit that I want to trust you. And yet, I tend to be very cautious in my relationships with people."

He laughed, a deep, rich, rolling laugh that filled the small yard. Down the street, a dog started to bark. "That is something I have known since I first sat beside you in the restaurant, my dear. I see you as a bit of a challenge!"

Her grin was a bit lopsided as she tilted her head and gave him a critical look. "Is that all I am—a challenge? If that's the case, perhaps I should not fall too easily—or at all."

"My dear woman, you do not see the incredible sexiness that pours from your very being, do you? Men turn their heads to look at you when you pass by and you do not even see it."

She shook her head. "It's getting pretty deep out here. I'm a married woman. Any sex appeal I might have had got turned off for all but one man when I said, 'I do.'"

"Ah, but there is where you are wrong, my dear." He held up a hand to forestall her protest. "My friend David has tamed you into turning off much of your...flirting? Is that the right word?" He didn't wait for her answer, but continued. "But at your core, there is a wanton that begs to see the light of day. It is her I saw in the restaurant, struggling against the walls you throw up so no one gets close. You use the excuse of caution to keep the wanton in her place."

Damn the man! How did he see all her tricks? She turned away in dismay.

"Taming that sexiness is a challenge most men could not meet."

"Well, you're right there." There was more bitterness in her voice than she intended as her mind flashed to her Saturdays, bound by David's hand. Suddenly those times seemed bland and uninspired. What she wanted was so much more than just bondage. But how much more?

"You want something your husband cannot give you in the bedroom."

Lissa leapt to David's defense. "He's a good man. He binds me when I ask him to."

Richard shook his head. "But he does not understand it."

"He does it because he loves me." Her chin jutted out as she found herself defending her husband's mostly mediocre lovemaking.

"Of course he does. But that does not mean he understands that bondage is more than just tying your body."

She swallowed hard. He was talking about slavery again.

"And that is what scares you now, correct?

Richard's almost nonexistent accent popped up occasionally in his choice of words or in the way he said a particular phrase.

"Yes, you are correct," she replied, defiance building in her heart as she half-heartedly mocked his formal turn of phrase. *Please let him bulldoze these walls.* Her silent plea echoed in the stillness of her soul. She *was* a challenge; she knew that. Her independent streak would let her be nothing less. Was Richard man enough to break through?

Tenderness filled his heart as he watched her independence war with her need to sexually submit. In time, she would come to understand she could have both. He smiled and brushed an errant strand of hair from her cheek as he considered how to convince her.

The kindness in his eyes and the gentleness of his touch melted a little of the barrier she had hastily resurrected. But when he spoke, his words confused her.

"Have you not realized yet, in a true Dominant/submissive relationship, that it is the submissive with all the power?"

"How so? I would be giving up whatever power I have to you."

"By choice only. I cannot force you. There are laws against a man forcing a woman to be tied and used against her will. You must come to me willingly."

"Yes, I understand that. But in doing so, don't I give up power? I cannot both give it up and have it at the same time."

The moon rose over the trees, its light spilling onto the tiny deck, illuminating the dark pools of Richard's eyes. Mystery surrounded him. His trimmed black mustache and goatee gave him the look of the devil himself. The thought of being tied and at the mercy of such a rogue aroused her and made her juices flow, soaking her panties. She waited for his explanation even as her head swam with the realization that she did want this man to dominate her, and she wanted it badly.

"You do have both at the same time." Quiet in the moonlight, his voice was seductive in its power. "You give up the power, but can take it back with only a single word. I cannot go further than you allow. You hold the power to determine what I can—and cannot—do to you."

Apparently without purpose, Richard's fingers skimmed over Lissa's bare arm, idly tracing a figure on her skin. His touch raised goosebumps in the night air, setting her body tingling with anticipation. She swayed as he came nearer, raising her face to him, desiring his kiss.

And when his lips closed over hers, she tasted the sweet wine they shared, and inhaled the scent of him deep into her soul. His arms encircled her, embracing all that she was. Of their own volition, her arms came up to hold his broad shoulders. This kiss deepened and her fingers dug into the hard muscles hidden under the black linen shirt. And when Richard's tongue brushed lightly against her lips, she opened her mouth, letting him possess her in a way she had never been possessed before.

His tongue penetrated deeply, flicking over her own, around it, assaulting, then caressing her mouth. The world did not exist. Only the touch of his tongue as he claimed her mouth, and she willingly gave up possession.

And when he pulled away, his eyes smoldering with controlled passion, Lissa knew she would lie down right there for him if he commanded it.

"Your body is mine, Melissa. Say it."

Without hesitation, Lissa accepted the inevitable. "My body is yours, Master Richard. I want to submit to you."

* * * * *

David looked at his watch, then looked again. "Holy cow! Do you realize what time it is?"

Adora shook her head. The two of them had been talking for hours, exchanging stories of their childhoods, trading recipes for favorite dishes, holding hands the entire evening. David felt moved by this woman in a way he'd never felt before. She was enticing and erotic, yet somehow as comfortable as an old worn-in sweater. Their dinner had ended around 7:30; it was now almost midnight.

"Our spouses must be getting along, or we'd have heard from them both." There was a lilt of humor in Adora's voice. She, too, had enjoyed the night's conversation. She felt as if she could very easily spend time with this man and tell him all her secrets.

With a start, David thought of Lissa's earlier reluctance about this night. Since sitting down to speak with Adora, he hadn't given her another thought. Guilt set in, and it showed on his face. "We'd best go find them, I suppose."

She placed her hand reassuringly on his arm as they stood. "Your wife is a strong woman and my husband is considerate. I suspect they have forgotten us just as we have forgotten them."

David nodded, trying to let her words ease his conscience. Still, his contrite look remained as the two of them headed back through the swinging door to find the others.

The moon had long since gone behind the approaching storm clouds and the temperature had turned a bit chilly. But that had not stopped Lissa and Master Richard in their conversation on the deck. When Adora and David peeked through the door, they found the two in a very animated discussion about feminism and how it related to the submissiveness Lissa warred with. Richard was laughing his deep, barrel laugh and Lissa had obviously just finished some particularly vehement statement; David saw her pound the table with her fist. But the light from the candles the two had lit illuminated her face and he could see she wasn't angry, but passionate. It was a look he had not seen in some time.

For a moment, a flash of jealousy crossed his heart, but then was gone. He had nothing to be jealous about. Hadn't he just spent several hours conversing with a beautiful woman and feeling similar passions building inside of himself? How could he not want the same thing for his wife? By the time he and Adora were on the deck, the green-eyed monster was gone.

"Well, you two seem to have found some things to talk about!" He walked over and leaned down to kiss Lissa, very aware that he was reclaiming his property by doing so.

She nodded, accepting his light kiss, wondering if his lips had kissed Adora's this evening.

"We did, my friend, we did." Richard stood and put his arm around his own wife's waist, giving her a fond smile as he did so. "Your wife is a woman of many opinions!"

"I told you she would be hard to tame." He put his arm around Lissa's waist in a move that unconsciously mirrored Richard's. The little squeeze he gave her let Lissa know he was teasing. Little did he know just how right he was. No matter how much her soul might want it, her mind kept getting in the way. There were just so many issues!

And Richard had dealt with every one of them in a calm and rational way. One by one, he dismissed her arguments with countering opinions he then backed up with her own feelings. Every wall Lissa threw between them in her fight, he took down, not with a battering ram, but with faultless logic. And in the end, she knew there could be only one outcome; she would fall completely into the subjugation of his will.

While she would have liked some time to talk again with Adora, it had gotten quite late. Goodbyes were said; David kissed Adora tenderly on the lips; Richard kissed Lissa's hand in an eloquent farewell gesture. With a small flourish, they were gone and David and Lissa were alone together once more.

* * * * *

David and Lissa lay side-by-side in bed, both exhausted; neither one tired. The evening's stresses allowed neither one to rest just yet. David was haunted by the dispassionate recitation Adora had given him of her past; Lissa was preoccupied with the way Richard had commanded her and how she had complied with his few simple requests. It wasn't until the two were in bed that David broke the thoughtful silence that stretched between them.

"So what do you think?"

"I have to give him credit, David. The man is incredibly intelligent."

It was not what he expected her to say. But then he smiled in the dim light filtering in from the streetlight outside. Lissa would never submit to a man less intelligent than herself. His appearance might be what caught her eye; his intelligence kept it.

"Oh?"

"He argues well. No matter what I threw at him, he was able to counter with a logical argument of his own. And he never tried to intimidate me. All that power he exudes...yet he used persuasion instead of force."

"You knew he was trying to seduce you. Sounds like he succeeded."

Lissa remembered the taste of his lips on hers. The rush of blood, the pounding heartbeat. Yes, she had to admit it. He most certainly was succeeding. Her breath quickened at the memory.

"What..." Her voice cracked. Clearing her throat, and calming the memories, she tried again. "What about you? Did things go well?"

In his mind, David again saw Adora in the soft kitchen light, her face alternately lit with anger, with hurt, with tenderness. "She was raped as a child."

"What?" Lissa sat up and faced him.

David nodded. "It was pretty brutal. I think she's looking for a refuge."

"Isn't Richard her refuge? Or is he part of the problem?" Lissa's heart sank to think her handsome Gypsy king might also be insensitive to his wife's past.

"He's not part of the problem. He sees it clearly. He told me she considered herself dominant, but he thought she wasn't."

"Adora told me the other night she and Richard both were dominant."

David nodded as Lissa lay back, pulling her over to him so he could hold her as they talked. With companionship borne of long association, their bodies melded, spooning into one another without thought.

"They are both dominant. Well, he is, anyway. Apparently that's how she approaches men now, because of the rape. But I don't think she is."

"You think she's submissive?"

"I'm not sure. But I'm pretty sure her dominance is just an act."

Lissa's curiosity got the best of her. "Do you want to go to bed with her?"

David looked down at his wife, her head nestled on his arm. When he did not answer right away, she turned her face upward; he hugged her a little tighter.

"It's all right, David, if you do. That's what tonight was all about, wasn't it?"

"Yes, then. I want to have sex with Adora. Are you sure you're all right with that?"

Lissa nodded, not trusting her voice. The two of them stood on the cusp of a very important step in their lives; the momentousness of it took her breath.

"What about Richard? Do you want to have sex with Richard?"

Her voice squeaked and she had to say the word twice, but she managed her answer. "Yes. Yes, I want to have sex with Richard."

"I guess our next step is letting them know that."

"How do you do that? I can't exactly see myself calling Adora and saying, 'I want your husband to tie me up and fuck my brains out.' That's a bit awkward."

"Let me talk to Richard and we'll see where this goes."

Chapter 4

Lissa left the details to David and Richard. The thought of being treated as a piece of property was a tremendously erotic thought. So when David informed her that Saturday night they would be forgoing their normal routine, her acquiescence was swift. And when he further informed her that Adora would be coming to the house and that Lissa would be going to visit Richard alone, her heart started a tattoo that threatened to make her come right there.

"Are you sure we're ready for this?"

"Lissa!" David's exasperation exploded in that one word. What did the woman want? First she'd been quietly accepting, then edgy, then giddy, now she was back to reluctant. He couldn't keep up with her moods. Especially not when the spousal switch was to occur in less than half an hour.

"You don't need to sound disgusted with me." She knew her emotions were out of control, and she didn't like it one bit. Normally she was the calm, rational one. But this situation had her tied in knots like she'd never felt before. When she was with Richard the other night, it had seemed so right. But in the cold light of day, her morality flew up in her face and made her question herself all over again.

"I'm nervous and I want some understanding, not your anger." She slammed the brush she was using on her hair down onto her dresser.

"Lissa, look, I'm not angry." David left his shirt half unbuttoned and came over to her. Adora would be here any moment and he wanted Lissa gone before she arrived. In the mood Lissa was in right now, his wife might throw the other woman out before she even got her foot in the door.

"Well, you certainly sounded like you are." She wasn't being fair to David and she knew it. But she couldn't help the petulance in her voice.

"Do you want to call this whole thing off? Because if you do, this is the time to say so."

She turned around and put her arms around his shoulders, apology in her voice. "David, I love you. And I don't want to hurt you."

"Are you telling me you're afraid that you'll fall in love with Richard?"

"As you've already fallen in love with Adora?"

He blustered and tried to pull away, but her arms only tightened around his neck. "Lissa, I love you, not her."

"David, I am not an idiot. Nor am I blind." She caressed his cheek. "You have a lot of love to give, I understand that. I don't mind sharing you, I suppose, but what if I do?"

David looked confused.

"What if I do fall in love with Richard? What does that do to us?"

"Nothing." He was adamant. "And I'm not in love with Adora. I like her, yes. I want to have sex with her. Nothing more."

Lissa smiled sadly. She wanted this night as much as he did, and yet, she already saw consequences neither of them could control. "There's only one thing I know for certain, David. When the night ends, we will be very different people than we are right now."

He kissed her on the top of the head and broke away. "Nonsense, Lissa. One night of sex does not change an entire person." He paused. "Or are you telling me you think you'll be changed?"

"I don't know. I guess. That's part of my anxiety. I have a pretty strong self-image, you know."

David grinned. "I know." He went back to his dressing, pulling on his shoes and tucking in his shirt.

"But will I still, afterward?"

"Why wouldn't you? Lissa, you're strong, independent, and beautiful. Richard is attracted to you. Enjoy the desires you've always had. When you come home, I'll be here."

"You're right. I'm just jumping at 'what ifs' and 'maybes.' Hand me my dress?"

He held it up for her so she could slip her arms into the light summer sundress. The spaghetti straps fell to her shoulders and she tugged the dress with its tasteful little flower pattern into position. A strapless bra underneath kept her somewhat ample bosom from bouncing around; her naughty side had her once again sporting a thong. Other than that, she was wearing only her fears mixed with desire.

David kissed her at the door and sent her on her way. Even after she was gone, he felt no nervousness. That surprised him. When he and Lissa first had sex after the wedding, he'd been as nervous as a schoolboy on the very first day of school. Tonight, however, there was a difference. Tonight he knew what he was doing and why.

Stepping into the guest bedroom, he glanced about to make sure all was ready. That was one thing Lissa had insisted on. "No sex with another woman in my bed. That's *our* spot," she had declared when he first told her the arrangements. He saw her point and agreed. The guest room needed to be cleaned out anyway. Now it was prepared with fresh linens and candles set strategically about. Even the summer night cooperated, sending a warm breeze in through the open window to scent the air with fresh beginnings.

The sound of a car in the drive gave him a momentary qualm. What if Lissa was right? Could this night change them both? Dismissing the thought, he leapt down the stairs and had the door open just as Adora stepped onto the porch.

"Resplendent as always."

She looked up and smiled at his compliment. If anything, she was more modestly dressed this evening than she had been in their previous encounters. Her sleeveless turtleneck enhanced her long neck and thin torso, tapering over her hips where it just covered the waist of her jean skirt. Buttons along the side of the skirt ran from her waist to just above her knee, although the skirt hung almost to her ankles. Somehow the flash of leg David saw was more erotic than seeing the entire beautiful appendage.

Adora's voice, soft and alluring, pulled his attention to her exquisite face. "Thank you. You are looking quite handsome yourself."

Tempted though David was to lean forward and kiss her, he held back. No use giving the nosy neighbors something to discuss. Instead he held open the door and waited for her to pass through before closing it quite firmly behind him.

"May I get you a drink of some sort?" He didn't need one himself, but to not offer would be rude. Couldn't very well say, "Well, glad you're here, let's go have sex". In truth, he liked taking it slow. Go too fast and neither party would be satisfied. And if they never even got to the sex part? Well, that would be all right, too. Although he wondered if Adora would be willing to suck his cock. All week long that fantasy had teased him, but after hearing her story last week, he would never push her to such a thing.

"Thank you. Water would be fine."

"Water it is!" David gestured to the living room as he headed into the kitchen to get the drink. He made it to the sink, the glass in one hand, the other hand on the faucet when he felt her hands slide around his waist.

"We could just get down to business, you know." Her sultry breath tickled his ear as her hands slid downward, caressing his cock through his pants. He felt her body slither along his backside; his cock grew hard immediately.

"Whoa, Adora. Don't you want to take some time?" He struggled to turn around at the sink and face her.

"Why? This is what you want, isn't it?" Her fingers reached for his belt, pulling the loose end out of the loops and beginning to unfasten it.

"Stop this. No, this isn't what I want." He batted at her hands while trying to find a place to set down the still-empty glass.

"Yes, it is. I saw it in your eyes the very first night we met. In the diner. I showed you my ass that night, remember?"

"How could I forget? Of course I remember." His belt opened and he twisted to the side, trying to angle himself away from the sexy woman.

"Then let's have sex. Hot..."

Adora's hand squeezed David's balls through the thin fabric of his pants.

"Wet...."

Her breath caressed his neck.

"Juicy...."

Her tongue snaked out to flick his earlobe.

"Sex."

She leaned into him, her hands sliding into his waistband and down along his rump to grab his ass cheeks with her fingers as she pressed her pert breasts into his chest.

David closed his eyes as his head swam. Her scent was wonderful, overpowering; she wanted him. His cock responded, growing uncomfortable in the bindings of his pants. With an effort, he grabbed her wrists and pulled her hands off his ass and out of his pants and held them before her.

"Adora, stop this now. This isn't what you want and you know it."

Her eyes flashed. "I want to bring you to your knees and make you beg me to let your cock be satisfied. I want to see you crawl on the floor in agony from a cock so hard it hurts."

Even as she said the words, there was a flicker in her eyes and David spied the truth Richard had alluded to. It was her husband's opinion that the forward, dominant woman was just a protective wall Adora hid behind; few were ever privileged enough to even peek at the little girl that cowered inside. Richard had never been able to tame the wilder side of Adora long enough to allow the hidden side of his wife to emerge. But David caught a glimpse of that little girl in the flash of her challenge. Could he bring her out?

"Adora, no." He held her wrists firmly, shaking them for emphasis.

This time anger flashed in her eyes. "Let me go." She struggled to get her hands free and David immediately released them. She took a step backward and glared at him. "If you do not follow my orders, you do not truly want me."

"That's not true and you know it." David remembered Richard's words of warning; this woman had already had her way with several men. He was determined not to be among the "tamed".

For answer, Adora turned on her heel and headed out of the kitchen. David debated; was she crying out for him to follow her? Should he remain where he was? He chose the former, moving slowly from the sink into the hall as he zipped his pants.

Adora stood, her hand on the doorknob of the front door, but it was obvious to him that she was hoping not to open it. She studied him defiantly as he walked down the short hall, but said nothing.

Neither did David. He simply crossed his arms and leaned against the archway to the living room and watched her. He saw the indecision cross her face, then become resolute. She yanked open the door.

"If you go home, you'll only walk in on Richard and Lissa. Or do you intend to call off their affair as well?"

When she hesitated, a small feeling of gratification tried to bloom in his chest; he ignored it. No victory had been won yet.

"You're welcome to stay here, even if I won't have sex with you on those terms." She hadn't fled yet. He took that as a good sign.

"I suppose you want sex on your terms." She wasn't looking at him, her body tense. David realized she still might take flight.

"If we have sex at all, yes."

She cocked her head at him, a puzzled look on her face. But she did not leave.

"I know in the past you were a dominatrix." He held up his hand to stave off her protests. "Richard and Lissa both told me."

"I *am* a domina; I have brought men to their knees before." She slammed the door shut and stood with her chin raised and her eyes flashing.

"But you do not want to bring me to my knees." He stood and took a slow step toward her, keeping his hands to his sides.

"I want to bring all men to their knees."

"Not Richard." He took another step. "And not me."

She looked for pity, defiance, or anger in David's face. All emotions she'd seen in men before. None of them existed in David's eyes. Only kindness and...understanding? Adora took a step backward in confusion.

David halted. When he was a child, he had captured a wounded and frightened feral cat that lived in the meadow behind his house. Patience, slow moves, a soft voice were all techniques he used to help him catch the cat and tend to it. But his mother later told him that those were only the externals. The cat had come to him and allowed David to help it only because it had come to trust the honest spirit inside the boy. He wanted Adora to see that honesty now.

Slowly, he raised his hand, palm up. "Friends first?" He waited. She had to come to him. If she couldn't make the first step from behind her dominatrix wall, then it was all over.

Still Adora hesitated. After a long moment, she put her hand in his, her eyes narrowed, watching David's reactions.

He was careful to allow no sense of triumph to show in his manner or his eyes. He saw his way now. Adora and the wild cat were one and the same. Never trusting, never allowing anyone to get close. Too used to having to fend for themselves, they built walls of anger and defiance around them. The cat hissed and clawed, Adora retaliated for her past by making men crawl.

He led her to the dining room table and pulled a chair to the side for her. Her look was again puzzled. Good. Keep her slightly off balance. In truth, he wanted to keep the playing field level for the two of them; the couch afforded a place to snuggle, but she wasn't ready for that yet. The armchair and stool had too much symbolism. No, the equality of the dining room chairs with a table beside them was much safer. He pulled his chair from the head of the table and placed it before hers, then sat down.

* * * * *

Lissa circled the block twice before gathering enough courage to pull into the driveway. Was she really driving to another man's house for no other reason but to have sex? It seemed so out of character.

And yet, the steps that had led her here were logical: she wanted to be bound and used, Richard attracted her, he and David had agreed, and here she was. Simple.

Richard opened the door to greet her and once again his appearance took her breath away. Tall, dark and handsome, just like the fairy tales. His broad chest covered in his habitual black shirt, gave her just a peek at the mat of hair underneath. And that little Superman curl over his forehead didn't hurt. The goatee gave him a mysterious air, the cut of his clothes attested to his power. Or would that be wealth? She stopped noticing when he took her hand and led her inside.

The exotic living room, with its throw pillows and pair of armchairs, was no different than her last visit. But Richard stopped her at the entryway, turning her to face him.

"Melissa, we both know why we're here tonight. But there is much more groundwork to be laid between the two of us before we have intercourse."

"We're not having sex tonight?" At first shocked by the man's forthrightness, she then didn't know if she were more relieved or disappointed.

Richard's booming laugh filled the room. "I never said that. I implied we might not have intercourse. There is a great deal of sex we can have before we get that far."

She grinned and nodded. There certainly was. Her shoulders relaxed and when he led her into the kitchen to get them drinks, she followed a little more at ease.

Richard offered her a soft drink, with an explanation. "We both need our wits about us. I never drink alcohol when I have a sub in my care. And I want your experiences unclouded as well."

She accepted the soda and sat at the table when he pulled out a chair for her. The kitchen was non-threatening enough, she decided as she sipped her drink and tried to think of something clever to say. Nothing came.

"So tell me, Melissa. When did you first learn the word 'submissive'?"

She set the glass on the table as she thought over the question. "I'm not sure. I've always been intrigued by being tied up during sex. I told that to David both before we were married and afterward. But he saw it as just a game and I didn't. I guess it was about the time I figured *that* out that I also realized it wasn't just the bondage. There was something else I wanted, too."

"But at that time you had no name for it?"

"Right. I don't know, maybe I read too many romance novels as a teenager." She assumed a dramatic pose. "Where the hero tears off the woman's clothes and presses his kiss on her lips despite her protestations." She dropped the pose and laughed. "Those scenes always struck a chord in me. And I can't be the only one, look at how many women buy those books!"

Richard smiled at her antics. "I'm sure you are not alone. So how did you find the right word?"

"The internet came along. I started looking under the word 'bondage' at first, always when I was alone; I didn't want David to know."

"Why not?"

"I thought he wouldn't understand. I don't want to hurt him. I love him very much."

"But?"

"But you already know. He's vanilla—a word I learned about the same time—and I'm not. I'm submissive." Somehow she managed not to blush at the admission.

"Then stand before me, Melissa."

Her first real order. Uncertainty suddenly fluttered in her stomach; she disregarded it and rose, coming around the corner of the table to stand before him. Now she could not curb the deep red blush of her cheeks.

"Now that wasn't so hard, was it?"

She grinned self-consciously. "Not too hard."

"Give me your hands."

With less hesitation this time, she held her hands before her.

Richard pulled a set of handcuffs out of his pocket. Never taking his eyes off her, he fastened first one side, then the other around her wrists.

Lissa could not take her eyes from the cuffs. Silver light flashed from them as she twisted and turned her arms, testing them. Police handcuffs. The kind that only came off with a key. Bound in front of her, she could still use her hands to fend him off if she chickened out, although the cuffs hampered her movements. Her pussy clenched and surged beneath her dress.

"Please take your seat again, Melissa."

Each order got easier to obey. She backed up the few steps needed and sat down, her cuffed hands resting uncomfortably on her lap.

"What are you thinking, my dear?"

What was she thinking? Her mind was in a tizzy. "I'm not sure," she confessed.

"Are you wet?"

She knew what he meant. "Yes." She dropped her head as her cheeks flamed again. A lock of hair fell in her face, and she started to raise her hand to brush it back, but both hands rose, bound in the handcuffs. Her stomach clenched and she stifled a whimper of arousal as she carefully set her hands back on her lap.

His fingers lifted her chin. "You have nothing to be embarrassed or ashamed about, Melissa. Your arousal makes you even more beautiful than you already are."

The compliment only deepened her self-consciousness. But she kept her head up as his hand dropped away and she met his eyes with determination.

"You like how they feel against your skin? Tell me what you are thinking."

His gaze intensified and she felt a small thrill. Closing her eyes, she took a deep breath to steady herself, letting it out with a rush before opening them again. "I am, first of all, a bit surprised that I'm sitting in a man's kitchen with my hands cuffed while carrying on a conversation with him. That's a bit disconcerting." Lissa smiled shyly and continued. "The cuffs are cold, but not a lot." She twisted her arms again, feeling the bondage of her wrists. "And even though the thought that I can't get loose...umm...arouses me, it scares me as well."

Richard beamed. "Excellent! Now that was a worthy answer, my dear. When I ask you, I expect you to tell me all that is in your head at that particular moment. Only by sharing that will you give me what information I need to continue. Do you understand what I am telling you?"

Lissa nodded, relaxing and smiling under his compliments. He was seducing her and she wanted to be seduced. She had been worried he would be demeaning and harsh; she found instead a man intent on truly understanding her.

"I am going to test your willpower. Your hands are to remain in your lap. Do not move them from where they are now."

She nodded her acquiescence. Somehow, knowing that he was testing her made it easier to submit. Richard stood to bring his chair immediately before her. When he sat, his knees lay beside hers, holding them in place. His scent wafted to her; a pleasant cologne that reminded her of cloves. The exotic scent of a Gypsy king. His approach made her heart beat faster but she did not move her hands from her lap.

Not even when his fingers traced along her cheek, exploring the curves of her neck with his touch and with his eyes did she move her hands, clasped tightly together in their cuffs. She raised her head as he traced along her neckline, wanting to give him better access. Although, when his hands pushed the spaghetti straps off her shoulders, her hands twitched out of habit.

Richard paused and she calmed them, raising her head again when she was ready. His fingers pushed the little straps down along her arms until each rested on her bent elbow. The neckline of the sundress also slipped down so that all that covered her was the strapless bra.

Why had she worn this thing? Why couldn't she have just gone with the whole 'bad girl' thing and gone braless? No, her independence had to keep throwing up roadblocks. And it wasn't even the kind that could be unsnapped. She had to wear an elastic sport bra to bind her breasts in. Now that bra was one more barrier between her desires and Richard's slow moving, sensual hands.

Richard did not seem at all bothered by it, however. He again lifted her chin to look into her eyes. "Tell me what you are thinking, Melissa."

"I'm thinking I'm sorry I wore a bra at all."

"Do you want it off?"

She hesitated. Didn't being submissive mean letting him do as he wanted? What did her desires matter? But Richard had ordered her to tell what she was thinking, so she answered, her voice barely a whisper. "Yes."

He caught her eyes with his again, and held her gaze as his fingers once again traced her shoulder line, along her collarbone to the small hollow of her throat, then downward to run along the tops of her breasts where they swelled, a small ridge of flesh not protected by the fabric barrier. Lissa did not even realize that she leaned forward in a silent entreaty.

But Richard did not remove the garment. Instead, his fingers brushed down over the fabric, finding her rising nipples and the fullness of her bosom. He was in no hurry. His very deliberateness would have her begging for him sooner than she thought possible.

His thumbs caressed her nipples; the elastic fabric stretched as those buds rose in response to his stimulation. Only when they could rise no higher did he change his touch, bringing his fingers up to the top of the bra. He slid his forefinger into the space created by her cleavage and brushed the skin of her breast with his knuckle.

What she wanted was to caress the backs of his hands, to urge him to pull down the bra. But she was not in charge here; she had an order to fulfill. With an effort, she kept her hands still.

Her effort was rewarded. Richard grasped the garment by the bottom and slowly pulled it down, revealing increments of her breasts at a time. Lissa felt her breasts swelling up and when at last the nipples popped free, she gasped. The bra fell around her waist and she was naked from the waist up.

* * * * *

David and Adora talked for over an hour. Taking pains to remain non-threatening, David had gotten Adora to talk more about the rape she lived through and what it had done to her. To him, it was obvious her dominatrix attitude was directly related to the incident. When she confessed she hated to be tied up because of that, David understood why Richard could not "tame" her. "Because Richard likes his sex a bit rough, the two of you are not compatible in that department, am I right?"

They still sat beside the dining room table as the darkness of the late summer evening descended. At some point during the conversation, David had taken Adora's hands; he held her delicate fingers entwined with his.

"Yes," she admitted, disengaging her hands to sit up and to pull her long hair back from her face. "I love

Richard, but we have not had sex together in quite some time."

This was an unexpected revelation. The sex he shared with Lissa lately had never been better. The vulnerability in Adora's face made his heart ache. He suspected a little tenderness now and she'd fall into his arms. But that wasn't what he wanted. He didn't want pity sex with the woman any more than she would accept it from him.

"Do you want to? Have sex with him again at some point?"

She tilted her head, considering. Finally she leaned back in the chair with an explosive sigh and a word David did not understand. When she saw his confusion, she giggled.

"My apologies. It was not a very nice word in a language I no longer speak. My frustration is showing."

David grinned. "My father knew a few words a friend had taught him in Italian. I suspect they meant the same thing." The light was getting decidedly dim, yet the mood was too fragile to risk losing by turning on the bright overhead light. And he'd taken most of the candles upstairs in his naïveté. Only the "good" candles were in their places on the sideboard in ornate silver candlesticks he and Lissa had been given for their wedding. They would do.

He waited to see if Adora would answer his question, busying himself with getting out matches and moving the candlesticks and candles to the table to give the woman time to think about what she wanted from her husband. Only once he was seated again, the soft, romantic light of the tiny flames throwing a circle of intimacy around them, did she make her reply.

"Yes, some day it would be good to do more than just lie in his arms. I would like to feel his caress again, the soft touch of his hands on my skin."

"He can't do that now?" How could one be married to a goddess such as this and remain apart?

She shook her head. "No, Richard's needs threaten to overwhelm him. He has not had an outlet for quite some time. I am hopeful that Lissa will be able to tame that in him."

David laughed out loud. "And here I thought Richard would tame her!"

"It will not happen all at once; their relationship will need time to grow, but I suspect your Lissa might be the one to ensnare the wild beast that he controls with expert precision. There is a rare quality about her I've not seen in any of his other women."

For some inexplicable reason, David's heart swelled with pride at her words of praise for his wife. "What quality is that?"

"The ability to totally submit, while still retaining her own identity."

"And is that a quality you also have?" David's voice was quiet.

"I don't know." She looked troubled.

"To submit means you'd have to let someone past all your defenses. You'd have to let them in and allow them to really care about you for you. Not for your beauty, or for your sexual prowess, or even for your intelligence. For you." His hand brushed her hair back where it had fallen to obscure her face.

"I cannot, David. I cannot let you in yet." He saw the tears in her eyes.

"I know, Adora. I know. But know that I am here should you decide it's too lonely in there by yourself."

The tears fell and David remained where he was, letting her cry. While his heart longed to take her in his arms and let her soak his shirt with her tears, he respected her need for distance; in time she might let him in. He had shown patience with a wild cat, he could have patience with the woman before him.

To give her some time, he stood and went into the kitchen to get her a tissue. The glass still sat empty on the counter; might as well get her that water she'd asked for before. He managed to get it filled from the tap when he felt her hands on his back again. Shutting the water off, he turned around.

Adora had dried her eyes and now silently took the glass from him, draining a third of it in one long pull. Setting it on the counter, she took his hands.

"Now, just because I cannot let you into that side of me, does not mean we can't both be sexually satisfied tonight, my dearest David."

There was no trace of the vulnerable woman he'd left in the dining room; but there was no trace of the dominatrix either. Only a very sexy, obviously horny woman stood before him.

"I have to admit, I wouldn't mind a little sex myself," he admitted grinning like a schoolboy.

"Uncomplicated, plain old sex. Shall we?" She pulled him up from where he leaned against the sink.

"I do believe we shall, my dear lady. This way."

With a short detour through the dining room to blow out the candles and pick up the matches, David led Adora to the guest room. He had touched the vulnerable girl inside; for tonight that would be enough. Now, he would deal with the woman grown.

*   *   *   *   *

The summer dress lay forgotten on the kitchen floor, the bra artfully dropped beside it. Only the thong remained where Lissa originally put it, and that scrap of fabric was soaking wet from the juices that continually flowed from her pussy.

Richard had taken her by the handcuffs and led her upstairs to one of the bedrooms. But that was a misnomer; there was no bed in this room. There was what appeared to be a rack of sorts, but no bed. Other odd accoutrements puzzled her, and Richard gave her time to consider them. Deftly, he removed her handcuffs, then gestured to the room at large. "Explore, my dear. Observe all you wish. But do not touch."

The warning was clear, as were the directions. Putting her hands behind her back, and clasping them so she would not inadvertently touch something, she examined the room and its equipment. Because the house was of Cape Cod design, the ceiling sloped on the far side; a wide dormer window, however, allowed plenty of ceiling space throughout.

To her left assorted implements hung from hooks imbedded in a pegboard wall. A set of leather cuffs with padlocks caught her eye; real ones, not like the Velcro ones David had used with her. Her heart beat a little faster. Several whips, including one very long and nasty looking one that had a very thin tail, hung like so many limp brooms. Quite a few types of painful-looking clamps, a bag of clothespins, several lengths and types of rope, and a few other items she could not identify also hung neatly from the pegs. The dampness between her legs increased dramatically, as did her heart rate. Did he intend to use all these things on her? And wasn't that exactly what she wanted?

Lissa continued her circuit. Richard had only turned on a small lamp near the door, so odd shadows made it difficult to discern some of the items in the room. Something large and rectangular stood in the corner, but since it was covered in a scarlet cloth of velvet, she could not tell what it was. Lissa clenched her fists behind her back to keep them from raising the cloth and taking a peek. Whatever was under there was taller than she was, but not by much. She passed it by.

The rack came next. Up close, she realized it wasn't really one of those medieval torture devices; no turnscrew adorned the end. Rather, it *was* a bed of sorts, made of strong plywood for the base. Eyehooks and holes were scattered at even intervals around the outside edges with a lever off to the side. The holes and hooks she understood, but she wondered what the lever was for. Glancing at Master Richard, she decided not to ask just yet.

Around the bottom of the "bed" and over on the other side of the room, she found three more strange shapes under more scarlet velvet cloth. Two were very oddly shaped—one long and bumpy, the other tall and thin— pressed fairly close to the wall. The last one was small and boxy with several more implements set on top of it, the uses of which she could not imagine, although her fantasies did try.

Her tour completed, she faced Master Richard again, letting her hands fall to her sides. Though fear and excitement mingled and made her stomach flutter, his calm demeanor and commanding gaze eased her fears a little, even as a part of her stood by in disbelief. Was she really going to let this man *use* any of these things on her?

"Very good, Melissa. You follow orders quite well."

His words of praise sent a small thrill through her, even as the independent side mocked her: *how dare you feel pleasure because you followed a man's simple orders?* That was the voice she wanted Master Richard to muzzle. Although she stood still, she willed him with her eyes to take her places she had only dreamed of.

"Tell me what you are thinking as you stand here, almost totally naked before me in a room designed for sexual pleasure?"

The words alone made her pussy twitch in expectation. "I'm wondering what a lot of these things are. Some of them I've seen before," she gestured toward the pegboard, "and some I have not." She inclined her head toward the "bed".

"Are you regretting your decision to come upstairs with me?" His dark eyes were penetrating; Lissa felt him touch that hidden center of her soul as he had several times since they'd met. Adora had called that essence her "wild mare" that, once tamed, would mean she had given away every part of her being to a man. For several heartbeats, she returned his gaze, aching for him to control that resistant spirit inside. Finally, she shook her head.

"No, I do not regret it at all."

"Melissa," Richard's smile was kind as he gazed down at her. "Do you still wish to submit to me? You must know by now, I want more than the submission of your body."

She did know it. And she wanted to give it. Desperately. "Yes. I know."

He stepped closer to her near-naked form, the hunger inside his soul tightly controlled. "I cannot force that part from you, you must give it freely."

In her exploration of the room, Lissa had grown comfortable with her nakedness, almost forgetting it completely. Richard chose to remind her of it, running a finger along her hairline, brushing her hair back from her face and over her shoulder, letting his finger meander down along her collarbone to trace circles around her bare breast. Like an animal trainer stalking a wild horse, he kept his movements slow and unthreatening. If he was right, this woman before him would be worth the wait.

Holding still was excruciating. His fingers meandered over her skin, and she wanted to push her breast into that powerful hand.

"Tell me, Melissa, do you still want to submit to me?"

"Yes!" The word ripped from the depths of her soul. "Please, yes. Let me be your lover, your toy to play with, your..." She paused, swallowed, and said the word, "Your slut."

His smile was not of triumph, but of understanding. Richard knew better than she did what she asked for. She would learn, in time. His finger still traced circles around her breasts; he changed the pattern now, his finger tracing ever-smaller circles, coming closer and closer each time to her very aroused nipple. Keeping his manner maddeningly casual, he regarded the beautiful woman before him.

"Has David ever bound these magnificent breasts?"

"No," she whispered, then cleared her throat and regained possession of her wits. "No. I tried once, but the rope kept slipping off."

"That meant you didn't have them tight enough." His hand dropped abruptly. "Turn around and put your hands behind your back."

She did as she was told, swallowing the lump that suddenly formed in her throat. Master Richard walked around her and Lissa saw him take the leather cuffs down from the wall, then finger a few coils of rope, before finally choosing one of thick cotton. He stepped behind her again and she felt the leather encase first one wrist and then the other. Two separate clicks as each padlock was locked on, then a third as the cuffs were locked together.

"Test them."

She did, pulling her arms apart, twisting them from side to side; she was firmly caught. Her thong received a fresh moistening as she realized she could not even bring her arms to either side. Convinced she could not escape them, Lissa sighed and smiled. This was exactly what she wanted. The independent voice did not speak.

Lissa felt Richard's hands on her shoulders, turning her around to face him. He pushed her forward so that her breasts hung down a bit, but her hair fell down to block her view. His view as well, apparently, for he lifted it and placed her hair along her back. The woman had such a beautiful, long neck he did not want his view of it obstructed. Someday, he would see that slenderness encased in a collar put on by his hands. That was, if he didn't scare her away tonight.

He pushed her into position as if she were nothing but an object; she held herself gingerly, her breathing shallow and did not fight him.

Lissa watched as Richard made a loop out of a portion of the rope and settled her left breast into it. With a deft pull, he tightened it and Lissa gasped as the sudden pressure encircling her breast caused an arousal that made her giddy.

"You like that, I see."

"Yes." Lissa could not control the raspy breathlessness of her voice.

"Good." In the confines of his pants, Richard's cock twitched; he ignored it. He had searched too long for a woman who could surrender to him; too many times he had been disappointed. The woman whose breasts he now bound, however, showed a remarkable ability and desire to submerge herself in submissiveness.

Adora was too fragile for his more aggressive sexual tastes, although he loved her tremendously independent spirit. But her demons kept him at bay, and neither of them found satisfaction in their lovemaking. He'd tried other women; some enjoyed his bondage, but wouldn't submit with anything other than lip service; others became too nervous or begged too much. There was only one Master in the room at a time. So far Melissa showed a wonderful fortitude and desire for his touch. A little flame of hope flared inside; the trainer flashed a carnal smile at his unbroken mare.

She chanced a glance up at him. His dark eyes smoldered with satisfaction and lust. A small smile played around his sensuous lips, lips she longed to have cover her own, possessing her mouth as he had before. He stalked her, played with her. Her pussy twitched as he manipulated her mind as well as her body, desiring her total submission to him.

Several times he circled the rope around her breast until it formed a small, constricting collar. Her breast swelled in the bindings, turning a light pink.

"Open your mouth."

Surprised, Lissa did so, and Richard placed the rope in her mouth. "Bite down," he instructed and she did so, holding the rope taut as he now made a second loop for her other breast.

She was part of her own binding, she realized as the rope got wet with her saliva. He purposefully was making her be a willing partner. All she had to do was drop the rope and the game would be done. She clenched it tighter with her teeth.

He noted the twinkle in her eye as he made her clench the rope taut. Once again his cock stirred; the little minx enjoyed what he did to her! Putting aside thoughts of what was to come, he concentrated on binding her body and soul.

Both breasts bound, they turned a pretty pink. Showing no emotion, Richard took the rope from Lissa's mouth, reinforcing her understanding that she was just an object for his use. Keeping both ends of the rope taut, brought them around behind her. She could not see what he was doing, but felt the rope cross her arms just above the elbow. The next thing she knew, her elbows were being drawn together, forcing her breasts into the confining collars.

Her knees almost buckled.

Her head swam as the blood in her body rushed to her pussy, which now twitched uncontrollably. A touch and she would come.

But Richard was no novice; he knew what he was doing, and what his actions were doing to her. He let the arousal run its course; peaking and subsiding without reaching a climax before he tied off the rope. She would come at his command when he willed it. And at no other.

A large hook hung just above where they stood; he threw the remaining length of cord over it and anchored Lissa's body to the ceiling.

While her feet were still firmly planted on the floor, Lissa felt slightly off balance; the rope tied to her arms would not allow her to fall, yet her arousal made it difficult to focus. Nor was Richard finished with her. "Open your mouth," he instructed her again, this time placing a gag between her teeth. Only a cotton scarf with a knot for the gag, but effective nonetheless. Once it was on, Lissa tossed her head, and worked at it with her tongue, but it was not coming off.

"Yes, my dear Melissa. You are quite helpless now." Richard perched on the low cube and watched her. "You are quite the sight to see, you know. I love to see you struggle against your bindings." His soft, seductive baritone caressed her spirit even as the words enflamed it. "Go ahead, enjoy the helpless feeling and know you can do nothing to stop me from having my way."

He was playing with her mind again. Even though she knew that, his words sent a panic through her. What was she doing? Why had she allowed this to happen? Frantically, she struggled against her bindings, turning and twisting, shaking her head as she tried to get loose. The more she fought, the more her juices flowed between her legs until they dripped down along her thigh.

And to see that man just sitting there, so obviously enjoying her predicament. Did he see her arousal as well? Lissa slammed her thighs together, suddenly embarrassed to have anyone know how much this feeling of being totally helpless, totally at his mercy, aroused the wild mare.

He let her struggle a bit more before standing and resting his hands on her shoulders. She quieted immediately, staring up into his eyes, pleading for release, but not a release from her bonds.

And he would give her release. Just not yet. To break an animal without breaking its spirit was something that could not be rushed. Melissa stood still before him, her breath calming as she sought his eyes.

She did not want him to ask how she was doing; he remembered her emphatic statement the last time they met. And so he did not ask. His hands cupped her bound breasts, ostensibly to check their warmth, in reality, to watch the effect his touch had on her. The rounded bulbs of stretched flesh were smooth under his hands; he had not tied them tightly this first time, but in a binding strict enough to produce arousal in her. And did it?

"Spread your legs for me, Melissa."

Tears sprang to her eyes as she complied. He would see her soaked thong and damp thighs. Humiliation turned her cheeks bright red.

One hand continued to cup her breast, his other traced through the broad cleavage made by the confining ropes, and downward to the top of her thong. A finger slid under the fabric, arrowing straight for her swollen clit. And when he touched it, she cried out her need through her gag.

He withdrew his finger immediately. "Is that what you want, Melissa? Do you want to come?" A teasing glint in his eye enjoyed her torment.

"Yes! Yes, please." Between the soaked gag and her desire, her voice was muffled almost beyond recognition. Yet her meaning was clear. Lissa's body sagged against the ropes as her weakened knees struggled to hold her up. "Please, Sir, please let me come." A tear escaped to trickle down her humiliated cheek.

"Then come for me, my slut. Come hard for me." Richard plunged his finger down past the fabric to sink deep into her pussy. His thumb rubbed against her clit and Lissa cried out in a pleasurable pain that dangled her on the edge of the world. The ropes took her weight entirely as she hung suspended in time.

"Look at me, Melissa, and give me your release."

She could not disobey the power in that voice. Forcing her eyes open, she stared into his eyes as her body suddenly heaved and convulsed. She screamed and cried out as wave after wave plunged through her body. And when she thought she could take no more, Richard pressed again on her clit and a second time she balanced on the border between pleasure and pain for an eternity before plunging again into the abyss.

And when he pressed a third time, she cried out for mercy. Her entire body shook from her orgasm; she had no strength left. With little space between them he had forced three powerful climaxes from her body. Never in her life had she ever had more than one. Exhausted, she let the ropes hold her upright as Richard pulled away his hand.

Vaguely aware that Richard was undoing her bindings, Lissa was content to float in the haze within her mind. When he picked her up in his arms and carried her out of the room, she put her arms around his neck and nuzzled her cheek against the fabric of his shirt. Only then did it dawn on her that he had yet to take his pleasure. When he placed her on the bed and pulled down her thong to expose her completely, her juices flowed again, knowing what came next.

* * * * *

If Lissa were a perfume, she'd be something spicy, David decided, whereas Adora would be a beautiful flower from the garden. Not a rose; that was too strong a scent, too delicate a flower. More like a peony, he thought. Needing the help of an ant to open the blossoms, but once opened, gorgeous and spectacular.

Adora's naked body lay beside him now. Her turtleneck was somewhere downstairs, her skirt was on a step someplace along with his shirt. They had run up here like two kids, scattering clothing as they went. His pants lay in a heap in the hallway; her panties not too far away.

There was a joyous abandon in the woman that David realized he loved. The ability to throw away the past and enjoy the present. If he had his way, someday she would never again be haunted by her history and this present happiness would be her permanent condition.

They had fallen onto the bed, their bodies already entwining. Now David sat up and pulled Adora's slender arm from beneath him.

"Don't want to break this—you might need it later on."

"For what? This, perhaps?" She reached down and firmly grasped his swollen cock. He felt it twitch in her hand, responding to the warmth of her grip. He did not intend to spend his entire evening comparing Lissa to this woman, but when Adora's hand turned sensuous and she slithered down along this body to kiss the tip of his cock, David knew he had found heaven.

"You like this?"

"It's wonderful. I never, er, that is…" He faltered as her tongue reached out to tease the tip.

Adora's head popped up in surprise. "Lissa has never done this for you?"

"I've never wanted her to. I couldn't ask that of my wife." He realized how demeaning that sounded and hastened to explain. "I mean, she's not…"

Adora laughed and little silver bells rang. "Stop there, David. You're going to, what is the American phrase—dig a hole for yourself'?"

He grinned. "That's the phrase all right."

"I would have thought she might have done this for you even without your asking. But some women do not like the taste of a man's cock." Her grin was mischievous. "I, however, happen to like it very much."

David couldn't help himself. "Do they all taste the same?"

"Have you ever noticed how two people can stand side-by-side and use the exact same ingredients to each make a pot of spaghetti sauce, and yet both sauces will come out slightly different? So it is with men."

As if that were enough explanation, Adora dove down and took a big, long lick of David's slightly softened cock to bring it back to full hardness. It worked. His cock swelled again, the purple veins standing out in low ridges along the shaft.

Adora flitted off the bed, her pert breasts barely bouncing as she did so. "Put your feet off the bed and sit up, this is a good position for me to play in. And I will make you come!"

There was no command in her voice, only instruction and since this was so new to him, David was willing to follow her lead. He sat on the edge of the bed and let his feet touch the floor, his cock at attention. Adora knelt between his legs, getting comfortable on the floor before reaching forward to cup his balls with her hand, kneading the stones in her fingers.

"These are also nice to suck on, you know," she informed him as she ducked her head down and pulled first one and then the other into her mouth. David gasped and fell back onto his hands as powerful tremors of carnal arousal coursed from his center. His cock throbbed as she studiously ignored it, concentrating on his balls.

Just as he thought he could not stand another moment of the sweet torment, Adora let each stone pop from her mouth, covering them with her hand so the air on his wet testicles would not adversely affect David's obvious need. She continued to massage them with her hand as her mouth now began to work magic on his cock.

Wet warmth surrounded him as the woman took the tip of his cock into her mouth. Her tongue swirled around the soft skin, dipping into the slit and teasing him until a bit of pre-cum formed. Scooping it out, she swallowed it down and David moaned in his haze of sexual pleasure.

Now her mouth really went to work, taking his long length deep into her throat, pushing her nose against his belly. His body responded of its own accord, thrusting up to meet her mouth, pumping against the back of her throat. Adora's lips were everywhere, at the base of his cock, then hugging the tip, then off and sliding along the outside letting her tongue tease him. His heart raced with the caress of her mouth on the velvety smooth skin of his cock. When once again her mouth covered him, the sight of her beautiful face looking up at him, eagerness in her bright blue eyes, those luscious pink lips surrounding his cock, he could not help himself. He reached a hand out to rest on her golden head, guiding her as he thrust deep into her mouth. With a groan, he pulled out as his cum shot forth; he watched it hit her in the face. She smiled as more and more sticky fluid came out, covering her with gloppy strings of white.

David stared at the sight of her, smiling and enjoying the fact that he had just come all over her face. But then his elbow buckled and he fell back onto the bed.

"Be right back."

He lifted his head enough to see a naked Adora lightly prance out of the room. Running water noises came from the direction of the bathroom and he dropped his head to the bed again, his softening cock still wet and sticky, his heart still pounding. He closed his eyes and enjoyed the sensations.

Something warm and wet covered his cock and he popped his head up; Adora knelt between his legs again, a warm cloth in her hand, cleaning him. Her face still bore his cum. She took care of his needs before her own. There was something deeply satisfying in that thought.

He got up onto one elbow and watched her; she said nothing, only smiling up at him from her position on the floor. Once she was satisfied that he was clean, she used the cloth to wipe her own face. With another grin, she took the cloth back to the bath.

When they entered the room, David had turned on only the bedside lamp; they hadn't taken the time to light his carefully preset candles. He grinned to see them still there, unused and unneeded. Shrugging, he left them alone. Pulling back the covers of the bed, he crawled in, leaving room for Adora when she returned.

Only another moment, and the two were snuggled together under the warmth of the sheets. Usually David helped Lissa to come first, otherwise he was too tired to continue after he came. Tonight, however, he did not want Adora to go home unsatisfied. Although lethargy threatened to overtake him, he fought it easily; Adora's hardened nipples pressed against his chest and he longed to taste them.

His hand enclosed one breast in his palm; so small each one could fit in a champagne glass. Didn't the French consider that a perfect breast size? David thought he read that somewhere. He certainly didn't mind it. His thumb flicked her nipple and Adora's intake of breath made him smile. Apparently he was doing it right.

Now it was his turn to slither down, his mouth coming to rest between her breasts. She turned over onto her back, her fingers entwined in his hair and he leaned forward, changing from his thumb to his tongue.

If men's cocks had different tastes, so did women's breasts, he decided. Her nipple was sweet and he closed his lips around it in a gentle kiss. Her body arched up to him so he let his free hand slide down along her flat stomach to play for a moment in the thatch of blonde hair that covered her mound. And when she arched again, inviting him to go deeper, he accepted the invitation, sending his fingers exploring along the slit that opened beneath them.

For several moments, he fingered her clit with his middle finger while the companion fingers pressed against her labia, rubbing those twin lips growing slick from her arousal.

David had never licked a woman to her climax; the idea had always seemed a bit repugnant to him. But that was before Adora had shown him what kind of magic a tongue could work. Did she not deserve the same favor she had done for him?

He slithered down the bed, positioning himself between her legs. Twin lips, wet and pink with arousal, urged his investigation. Parting those lips with two fingers of one hand, he inched his face closer. Her scent filled his nose, the fragrance both musky and light. Dipping another finger into the crevice, he drew out the creamy white moisture he knew he would find. Grinning at her when her head poked up, he stuck the finger into his mouth and tasted her.

He wasn't sure what he expected, but it wasn't the slightly salty, but quite sweet taste he now savored. David dipped in again, gathering her juices on his finger and tasting her once more. He cocked his head to one side as if considering.

"Well?" Adora's head, framed between her pert breasts looked undeniably beautiful in the light from the little lamp.

"Not bad. Not bad at all." David's grin turned wry. "I may need some help here. I've never done this before."

Adora rolled her eyes and gave a mock sigh. "Well, once I teach you, I hope Lissa appreciates what you have learned!"

David laughed and moved closer to her pussy, the lips still spread by his fingers. Slowly, he lowered his head until his lips brushed her mound. This was not something he wanted to rush. Leaving a kiss on the top of her mound, he worked down and around her pussy, his hot breath exciting her as he planted a trail of moist kisses along the groove where her thigh ended and pussy began. His mouth continued downward until his nose brushed against her crack, as his hold on her pussy lips changed to a caress of her clit.

The moan from above his head let him know he was doing it right. Continuing his sweet torment of kisses, he made his way slowly along the other leg, listening to her whimpers of desire. Only when his mouth drew beside her clit did he gather his courage for the move to the center.

First he just kissed the outside of the twin lips; the sweet, salty taste of her filling his senses. He wondered what she would do if he pulled one of those lips into his mouth; she gave out the most wonderful gasp when he did so. Encouraged, he sucked it hard before licking along the inside of it and letting it go.

"Oh, David...I'm going to come!"

He grinned and slid a finger inside her tight hole; he wanted to feel the muscles contract when she came. But still he kept his mouth on her, moving now to her clit.

Keeping one hand on her leg to keep her from bucking, he sucked her clit into his mouth while slowly pushing his finger deep into her. Adora bucked beneath him and David knew her climax grew close. Taking pity on her, he increased his tempo, his tongue flicking over her clit while his finger plunged in and out of her pussy.

His reward came when he felt her muscles contracting around his finger as she moaned from the depths of her throat.

As long as her climax lasted, he eased his finger in and out of her contracting pussy. But when she at last lay still, panting in the night, David gathered her into his arms and held her close. She clung to him, her body shaking. It was only after several moments, that David realized she was crying.

"Adora?" He brushed the golden hair from her face and tried to read her expression in the dark room. "Adora, what's wrong? Did I hurt you?"

She shook her head, a movement David felt rather than saw. At least it was a negative shake. "What is it, sweetheart?"

Taking several gulps of air, and hiccupping once, Adora finally came out from her hiding place in the crook of his arm.

"I didn't know it could be like that."

David was baffled. "Like what?"

"So...so...sensual and slow and...tender." She sniffled again.

Now he was completely confused. "But you've had men lick you before, right? Even Richard has taken you this way, hasn't he? I know he's into bondage and all that stuff, but he doesn't make you do that if you don't want to — does he?"

Again Adora shook her head. "You do not understand. I told you before. Richard does not 'take me' at all. We do not have sex."

"Because of his demons, you said." He remembered now.

She sighed. "I fell in love with him and we married. My...past...made it difficult for me to be intimate at all, but he was patient and very kind. He explained his preferences to me after a while and I agreed to try it. But as soon as he tied my hands, it all came back and I lost my mind for a while.

"We agreed that manner of sex was not something I would ever be able to do. I remember, he asked me that night what I would like to do to the men who raped me. I told him I wanted to humiliate them all, and make them beg on their knees. He laughed and told me there were actually men out there who would like that sort of thing. Male submissives.

"I found I enjoyed their submission. But always there was still an empty spot and the men moved on. Richard holds me and loves me, but we both have different tastes. Yes, men have 'licked' me before, but always at my insistence; they did not enjoy it and I relished that.

"But that's not the way with you. You offered. You cared about me and nothing else. Until tonight, I did not know there was yet another way."

She buried her face in David's chest as her raw emotions spilled over again. He held her tightly, caressing her back and kissing her hair to comfort her.

"My dearest Adora, I'm afraid this way is the only way I know. Richard and Lissa have a name for this style, you know."

She looked up at him in the darkness. "They do? What is it called?"

He smiled. "Vanilla."

* * * * *

Lissa still wore the cuffs, although they were not locked together. She remained on the bed, watching her broad-shouldered Gypsy king remove his clothing. Naked, he stood beside the bed and let her look her fill.

The mat of black hair that Lissa glimpsed before curled over his chest, coming down to a thin line that led her eye like an arrow to his cock. And when her eye fell on that glorious appendage, her mouth fell open in shock. Fully erect and the width of Adora's thin arm, his cock extended a full nine inches or more in length. The dark purple head pulsed with pent-up need. In spite of herself, Lissa pulled away.

Richard turned to pick up something from the bureau behind him; Lissa saw the padlock in his fingers when he turned back.

"Give me your hands."

She did so with only a slight hesitation. He locked her wrist cuffs together, then brought her arms up over her head and fastened them somehow to the headboard. Lissa tried to squirm around and see, but Richard sat beside her on the bed and she remained still.

"You have beautiful breasts, my dear one. So full, like ripe cantaloupe heavy in my hand." His thick fingers traced the indentations made by the rope. The marks would fade by morning, but for now the lines stood dark red against her skin. It had been his intention to have her taste him tonight, but the look of fear in her eyes when he showed himself to her changed his mind. She was not ready for that. Not yet.

He toyed with her breasts, caressing them, gently tweaking her nipples. "These are perfect breasts to surround a man's cock. And that's just what they are going to do tonight. Do you understand?"

She didn't. What did he mean? But before she could ask, Richard knelt on the bed and swung a leg over her, straddling her stomach. He placed his long, thick cock in her cleavage, grabbing each of her breasts to wrap around the shaft. His powerful hands squeezed her breasts, molding them into the shape he wanted; Lissa arched and provided him with a better angle as Richard began to ride her body, thrusting his cock through the opening made by her squashed breasts.

She could not take her eyes off the smooth tip of his cock as it poked through each time. Big, round, purple, the slit filling with white pre-cum, her lips parted unconsciously each time it came near.

"You have sucked your husband, yes?"

She shook her head no, never taking her eyes off his cock.

"Never? Not even tasted it?"

Again she shook her head as his thrusts increased in tempo.

No wonder she had been fearful. He was glad he had changed his mind. The thought of being the first man to come in her mouth brought him to his own fulfillment. His voice, raspy with his arousal, growled out his words more harshly than he intended them. "Then next time I will teach you how to take a man in your mouth. For now, wear the present I bring you." With a loud, wordless groan, Richard came, his seed spurting out all over Lissa's breasts. She raised her chin as more cum fell onto her neck. Warm and wet, she reveled in the gift he gave her.

Her eyes, the lids heavy with arousal, stared at him, slightly unfocused. Grinning wickedly, Richard reached behind him and touched her clit; immediately her body responded, electric fire jolting through her.

"It is as I suspected. You have a body built for coming, over and over and over. Come again for me, Melissa."

She did. With her hands bound above her and her Master's body straddling her waist, only her legs were free. She bent them, pushing herself into his hand as her body convulsed in another climax.

He watched her body buck beneath him, enjoying her "forced" orgasm. Melissa obeyed his commands in a manner different from the other women he had taken. Somehow she was stronger yet more vulnerable than the others. Stronger in her independence, more vulnerable in her heart. If the woman beneath him chose to give him her heart, for her it would mean total submission. Only time would tell if he was the one to tame that heart.

When her body stilled, Richard leaned forward and took off the cuffs, letting her completely free. He rose and left the room, telling her to remain where she was.

Unfettered and free to do as she pleased, Lissa did as she was bidden, content to remain where she was.

Richard returned with a warm cloth with which he wiped her body. She had not moved from her spot on the bed. Yes, this woman had definite possibilities. He fervently hoped things were going as well for Adora as they were for him. This woman before him had the makings of being a fine slave. Sliding onto the bed beside Lissa, he washed his toy. First her pussy, then the cum from her breasts and chin, scooping it all up in the cloth. Clean, she pulled the covers over her and snuggled in as he returned the cloth to the bath. When he joined her in bed and turned out the light, he reached over and pulled her close. For the first time, he let down a bit of his own guard as she awakened the protective side of his heart.

For several moments, Lissa just cuddled against him, enjoying the warmth of his skin and the softness of the thick, black hair on his chest. Exhaustion threatened to overtake her; never in her life had she come four times in a night, let alone so hard.

"Thank you for the use of your body tonight, Melissa." Richard's sultry voice was soft in her ear.

"You're welcome...Master." Her heart twittered to hear her voice say that title.

"You must only give me that when I deserve it." There was a slight admonition in his voice.

"You do deserve it. I do not bestow that title lightly."

Richard smoothed the hair from her face, tilting her chin up. "If I am your Master, then what does that make you?"

Lissa's heartbeat raced as she realized the implication. Less than two weeks ago, Adora had named Lissa's biggest fear: "*If you find a man who can tame the wild mare inside, there will be no part of you unclaimed by a man. Your entire being will belong to others.*" And yet tonight, Richard had gone a long way toward subduing her resistance.

She smiled as she considered the question. Quiet strength emanated from him, she felt secure in his arms in a way she never felt before. Almost shyly, her voice soft, Lissa gave him her answer. "That makes me your slave."

Chapter 5

David and Richard had already decided that the spouses would not spend the night at the other's house. So it was with great reluctance that eventually David roused Adora and Richard roused Lissa to send the wives home.

Lissa fervently hoped David did not want to talk about the evening. She still felt wrapped in a cocoon made of rope and blossoming hopes; the emotions were still too raw to share. Tomorrow would be soon enough.

David paced until Lissa's car turned in the drive; the women must've passed each other on the road. Still, those few moments seemed an eternity to him. Grateful for the night with Adora, still he wanted his wife beside him in bed.

She fell into David's arms, holding him tightly, grinning from ear to ear. The night had been special for both of them, she realized as his lips covered hers in a very welcoming kiss. He smelled faintly of flowers — Adora's perfume. Instead of making her jealous, it gave her a tingle inside. Had her husband's cock been inside another woman?

David smelled the clove scent on Lissa's skin, had the man put his cock into his wife somewhere? Did she bear any marks? He didn't ask any of the multitude of questions that spilled over themselves in his brain. He simply took her hand and the two walked up the stairs together to bed.

They didn't have sex; neither of them had the energy for it. But Lissa snuggled into David's arms, spoon-fashion, contentment settling on her like a comfortable old sweater. David wrapped his arms around his wife and fell asleep with his head buried in hair, the scent of spices filling his senses with dreams of peace.

* * * * *

They awoke, still spooned and very much in love. David grinned self-consciously every time Lissa looked at him; Lissa blushed each time David smiled. Like newlyweds who still are a bit shy of each other, they dressed and got breakfast. They showered and removed the scents of last night's lovemaking, returning again to their regular selves. Only when the two were seated at the table, their breakfast before them, did David finally broach the subject that had them both grinning like kids caught with their hands in the cookie jar.

"Did you have a good time last night?"

"Yes." Lissa giggled, a noise David hadn't heard in many months. "Did you?"

"Yes." He sipped his coffee.

"Good." She smiled and turned back to the paragraph she had already read three times, reading it a fourth. David's command interrupted her attempt.

"Okay, I can't stand it. Stand up and take off your robe."

"What?!"

"You heard me. Stand up, and get naked for me, woman."

Laughing she stood and struck a sexy pose as the robe dropped from her shoulders.

"Turn around."

Mystified, she did so.

"All right, you can put your robe back on and sit down."

Pulling the silk around her, she had to ask. "Mind telling me what that was all about?"

"Just checking."

"For what?"

"Marks."

She sat back.

"And what if there had been? Marks, that is."

"I would expect you to show them to me like badges of honor."

Her jaw dropped in surprise. "You would?"

David nodded, feeling a bit smug. Obviously she had not expected that answer.

"You wouldn't get all protective and concerned for my welfare?"

"Lissa, I know what you want, I'm not stupid. I just can't give it to you, that's all. Richard can. I am glad you bear no marks this morning, but I fully expect you to next time."

"Next time?"

"You do want a next time, don't you?"

For a moment, she sat in silence. She did, but did he? Well, one of them had to go out on the limb. "Yes. I do want a next time. And a time after that as well."

"Good." He paused. "So do I."

"Good." She grinned and waggled her eyebrows at him, jerking her head in the direction of the stairs.

David laughed. "Come on, woman, forget breakfast, and put that body where your mind is."

Laughing, he chased her up the stairs. She had a lead on him, however, and made it to the room with enough headway to drop her robe and strike a reclining, sensuous position on the bed. Only her gasping for breath broke the sexiness of her pin-up pose.

David paused in the door, his robe unfastened, his cock hard and ready. The bed still bounced from his wife's leap upon it. She grinned at him now, her hair artfully draped over the arm that held up her head. Shapely curves from the height of her shoulders to the valley of her waist to the rise of her hips tapered to the point of her beautiful toes. He whistled and shook his head.

"I am married to a vixen, for sure." Striding into the room, David dropped his robe on top of his wife's and slid onto the bed beside her, scooping her into his arms.

"Are we really going to have sex? It's not Saturday night, David," Lissa teased.

"We are. Right here in broad daylight, I am going to take my wife and make her squeal." He lunged for her nipple, sucking it hard into his mouth.

"David!" She squirmed in surprise.

He popped up his head. "See? Just like that!" He nipped at her nipple with his teeth and Lissa gasped.

"You are one sexy woman, Lissa Patterson."

She smiled up at him, rolling to push her body closer to his. "And you are one sexy man, David Patterson."

Their kiss of passion ignited the fires only banked from the night before. David's tongue sought Lissa's and danced in her mouth, entwining and dipping, caressing and tasting. Lissa's hands reached for David's cock, massaging and loving, warm and sensuous. Moving as one, David rolled her onto her back, her hands guiding him so that he could enter her directly. He took her in one thrust, plunging deep; she arched as he entered, allowing him access. Together they rode one another, their voices raised in concert as their passion grew. Two souls as one, their need grew stronger until it burst from both in loud cries of satisfaction. Their bodies convulsed, overtaken by the passion that ruled them until they collapsed in each other's arms, spent.

Afterwards, they agreed it was among the best sex they'd ever had with one another.

"Do you think our time with another couple had anything to do with that fact?" Lissa asked when David remarked on it.

"I think it might have." David lay on his back, his hands clasped under his head. Lissa fingered her breast, idly playing with the nipple David had bitten.

"So playing with someone else has made our own relationship stronger?"

"We were pretty strong to begin with, Lissa."

"I know you love Adora."

"Do you mind?" He looked over at his wife for signs of trouble.

Lissa shook her head. "Actually, I don't. I've decided it's very possible to love two people at the same time."

"Does that mean you've fallen in love with Richard?"

She considered a moment. "I love what he does to me and I find him very sexy. But I'm not sure I'm in love with him."

"I think that's only a matter of time. He's just begun to assert his dominance over you. Didn't you discover a time last night when you would have done anything for him? Just because he asked you to do it?"

Lissa looked over at David in alarm. "Yes." Her voice drawled the word out. How did he know?

"Could you have done that if you didn't love him?"

"I respect him, that's not the same thing."

"Respect is love in plain clothes." He looked over at her. "I did research the whole Master thing when you first told me that was what you wanted. What Adora and I share is less complicated than the dance of D/s between a Master and submissive. You will come to love him, Lissa. I'm prepared for that."

She rolled over and kissed him soundly. Her husband *had* actually read the sites she'd given him; he hadn't just skimmed them before deciding her choices were not his choices. Gratitude and love swelled inside her breast. "You are the most wonderful man in the world," she whispered.

Afterward, combing her hair out for the second time that morning, Lissa's thoughts drifted back to her conversation with David before the night's swap. Worry at that time had convinced her the time with another lover would change them both and she had been right. They were changed. But not in any of the negative ways that scared her. Where before they shared a love, now the two of them were even more committed to one another than before.

With that in mind, Lissa suggested another swap whenever David felt comfortable with sharing her again. Leaving the details up to the others, she once more settled into her normal daily routine.

Except she could not get the image of Richard's cock out of her head. In odd moments all week the sight of it would come back to her. Long, thick as her forearm, engorged with desire; Richard had not let her touch it and she knew that only added to her fascination. She never had the desire to suck David's cock, but she found herself wondering what Richard would taste like. Poking out of that thick nest of curly black hair, the man's cock dominated her thoughts.

"Richard and Adora have invited us for dinner Friday night. Shall I accept?" David cradled the phone in his hands as he called to Lissa, interrupting her reverie. With a guilty start, she set down the baster she'd been drying...and rubbing while she pondered Richard's cock yet again.

"Yes, go ahead." She double-checked the calendar. Friday night was tomorrow night and the calendar was currently empty.

David made the arrangements, hung up the phone and sauntered into the kitchen to find his wife.

"So is this dinner only?" Lissa's stomach did a small flip as she considered the alternatives.

"At this point, yes. But I want you to remain open to the thought of staying the night."

Lissa's tremulous smile belied her burgeoning excitement. "And will you stay as well?"

"No." David's casual air hid his own inner excitement at the proposal Richard had made. "I will definitely be coming home after dinner. But perhaps, not with you."

Lissa grinned. "You mean Adora."

David dropped the act and pulled Lissa into his arms. "Would you mind?"

"Staying overnight with Richard? I'd like that. If you don't mind, that is."

"This sounds so absurd! I can't believe we're doing this."

Lissa laughed. "Well, as far as other people are concerned, we're just two couples who enjoy each other's company and get together for dinner every week."

"Except where other couples play cards after dinner, we swap wives."

"Swap husbands," Lissa amended.

"Swap spouses," David agreed.

"Who knows? Maybe this time I'll have a bruise or two to show you." Lissa grinned and sauntered out of the kitchen, wagging her ass at him provocatively.

David watched her go, his cock hardening at the thought of sharing his wife with another man. Definitely there was something very erotic about that thought. Just as there was something tremendously erotic about the memory of Adora's lips around his cock. The remembered scent of her pussy floated past his nose and he sniffed deep. What would it be like to sink his cock into that glorious scent?

* * * * *

Lissa dressed just as self-consciously for their dinner this time as she had before. She chose a short jean skirt she hadn't worn in quite some time, accompanied by a summer pink short sleeve blouse that buttoned up the front. No sports bra this time, instead she opted for a front closure push-up type. The summer's heat was too hot for pantyhose, so she slipped bare feet into her sandals. And in a rash act of wantonness, she left her panties in the drawer.

David noted his wife's slightly slutty outfit, and only grinned in enjoyment. He remembered her wearing that skirt before they married; the view was as good now as it was then. Lissa's shapely legs lent themselves to a short skirt.

"Come here, woman!"

Lissa looked at David and grinned when she saw the appreciative look in his eye. Meandering over to him, an exaggerated sway to her hips, she stood before him and put her arms around his neck.

"You called?"

For answer, David only ran his hands down along her sides, feeling the outer curves of her bosom, the inner sweep of her waist, down along her perfect hips. He bent forward, letting his hands travel further; finding the hem of her skirt and running his hands up the backs of her thighs to cup her bare ass cheeks. David raised an eyebrow at her in mock scolding.

Lissa blushed, but did not drop her own challenging gaze.

David bussed her on the nose and slapped her naked ass playfully. "Perhaps one of these days it will be you who goes into a restaurant and shows her ass to a strange man."

A thrill made Lissa's stomach do another one of those flips. "I don't know if I could do that."

"I bet you could if Richard ordered you to. Not yet. But in the future?"

She shook her head and grinned. "Perhaps. But that's a long way off." Tucking her arm through her husband's the two headed out for the night's rendezvous.

* * * * *

The four sat in the exotic living room sipping soft drinks as if it were the most natural thing in the world to have two women reclining on cushions while their male counterparts sat in the overstuffed chairs. Lissa and Adora smiled often at each other, but made little conversation, content to let the men have their say. And when they moved to the dinner table and the men held out chairs for them, Lissa gave Richard as royal a nod as Adora gave to David. Lissa was beginning to understand the power of silence.

Richard watched the woman he would soon have to himself. She glowed under his gaze as if the heat of his look were the sun to her blossoming flower. And she had dressed appropriately for the evening, almost mimicking what she had seen Adora wear the night the four of them first met. Intuitively the woman had seen his tastes and knew what he would like, and then she had dressed that way for him. In the depths of his being, he was pleased.

Lissa felt his gaze on her as his eyes sought hers often throughout the meal. His neatly trimmed beard and mustache looked less threatening tonight, more elegant. And his face seemed as if even more tanned by the sun; a dark, swarthy king ready to take his not-so-reluctant slave girl.

As for David, he thought Adora grew more beautiful each time he saw her. The quiet demeanor she presented during dinner only served to whet his appetite for her conversation later. Last week she had briefly shared the scared little girl that lived inside her soul; would he be able to coax her out again this week?

And Adora simply smiled to see the dynamics at the table. The dinner conversation ebbed and flowed as it had before. David was a good friend for Richard, and Lissa smiled at her several times during the meal. They would have to get together for lunch sometime this week. Adora thought it would be nice to be friends with her husband's toy, the one who would tame his wild beast. Did she dare hope that Lissa would tame him enough? She would very much like to make love to her husband the way she and David had made love before.

For she had seen a difference in Richard this week. Less moody, less prone to growl. Of course, the same could be said about herself. She turned her attention again to David, the man whose cock had never been sucked until she wrapped her lips around him. That fact still surprised her. There was a patience about him, an understanding she hadn't seen in men before. She knew he loved her, but she was not quite ready to love him back.

As the dinner wound to a close, Adora stood at a prearranged signal from Richard and began to gather the dishes. Lissa stood to help clear. To her surprise, Richard also stood, and David followed suit. The four worked together to take the dishes to the kitchen and scrape and put away. Adora ran the water to wash and David and Lissa took up towels to dry; Richard put away. The conversation here flowed more freely; Adora and Lissa taking the opportunity to throw in their own zingers on occasion. Soon the chore was done and the next phase of the evening was set to begin.

"Melissa." There was a different tone to Richard's voice and Lissa's ears perked up. She draped her towel across the rack as she faced her Master, her cheeks blushing as she did so. It was one thing to behave as a slave before just him. It was something totally different to do so in front of her own husband.

Richard saw that. Gratified that her eyes showed she would do as commanded, he took mercy on her embarrassment in front of her husband. In a more gentle voice, he asked her, "Are you ready to forsake your husband's bed and submit to me for the time we have set?"

She swallowed hard and spared a glance at David to make sure he was all right with this. At his nod, she stepped forward. "Yes, Sir, I am."

"Then say your goodbyes to David and go upstairs and wait for me in our playroom."

She turned to David, who took her arm and led her to the bottom of the stairs. Richard and Adora remained in the kitchen. As the door swung shut, David pulled Lissa's chin up and studied his wife.

"Is this what you want? I can take you home if you'd rather."

"No, David. I want this. I really do. Take Adora home instead."

He leaned forward to kiss her before she departed. As his lips closed over hers, Lissa closed her eyes, leaning in toward his warmth and love. His tongue caressed hers for only a moment before he withdrew and gave her a wink.

That made her laugh out loud and she knew her course was true. "See you later, dearest husband of mine!" And with a flounce of her skirt and a flash of her ass, she disappeared up the stairs.

David grinned and turned as Adora and Richard joined him. With a smile, Adora put her hand in his and nodded toward the door. Richard placed his hand on his shoulder and nodded; with that, David took Adora home to spend the night.

Chapter 6

Once again David had equipped the guest room with candles; this time they would not go to waste. Full from Adora's delicious dinner, the two paused downstairs only long enough to get glasses of water before heading upstairs. While Adora settled herself contentedly against the pillows and bolsters of the bed, David lit the candles, throwing a romantic cast over the otherwise ordinary bedroom.

"You seemed to be more relaxed this weekend," David noted as he joined her at the head of the bed, pulling a few pillows into place against the headboard to give himself a comfortable place to recline.

"I was just thinking the same about you." Adora smiled and tossed her hair back over her shoulder. The candlelight caught the golden brilliance, making it shine like satin; David watched as her hair settled to gracefully frame the petite features of her face.

"Would you mind if I played with your hair?" He knew his request came out of nowhere, but he had a strong urge to run his fingers through those burnished tresses.

Adora smiled almost shyly. "I love to have someone brush my hair."

David took the hint. Lissa always kept this room supplied for guests; a spare brush and comb along with assorted clips and bobby pins were among the amenities she kept up-to-date in the room. David rose and collected the brush and comb; Adora threw her legs over the side of the bed and tossed her head to settle her hair along her back.

He knelt on the bed behind her. Despite her more relaxed attitude, David saw the residual tension in her tight shoulder muscles. Putting the brush and comb beside him on the bed, David simply placed his hands on the warm glow of her bare shoulders. For several breaths, he did not move them, not until he felt her body begin to relax under his touch.

Gently his fingers pushed into the muscles of her shoulders; his thumbs pressing deep as each moved upward along her shoulder blades. His reward was immediate: a deep sigh came from Adora's soul, along with a sudden relaxing of her shoulders.

"Oh, David, that feels so wonderful."

"Close your eyes, then, and breathe deep."

The muscles of her neck soon joined the relaxed state of her shoulders. Up into her scalp he worked, his fingers slowly pressing and rubbing away conscious thought. Her head dropped forward; her slow, rhythmic breathing soon moved in concert with the motion of his hands.

Gathering her hair in one hand, David picked up the brush and flipped it over so he could brush the underside of her hair with long, slow pulls from her neck outward to the tips. He watched the golden river fall from the brush, then reached forward to gather it up and brush along the length of it again.

She tilted her head back toward him now, silently inviting him to take her deeper. David complied, bringing the brush up to catch the wisps that floated around her face and capture them, slowly pulling the brush through her hair to settle in his hand; a straight ponytail of flaxen silk.

The slow rhythm mesmerized them both. Long, deliberate pulls in the candlelight, soft, sensuous gold in his hands, muscles turning to jelly under his touch. Her body sagged backwards into his as he pulled the brush through one last time. Setting the brush aside, he took her tiny weight in his arms, and bent to place a warm kiss on the exposed side of her neck.

She stirred, turning her head toward him, her lips parted; her breath shallow and quickening. He accepted her invitation, claiming her lips in a lingering kiss.

David eased her back on the bed, her body still enveloped in his arms as they kissed again. He could feel the hunger in Adora's soul as she hung onto him, her lips seeking the tenderness he provided. Lissa knew David loved both the woman he married and the woman he now held in his arms; he did not try to hide that love in the warmth of his embrace.

Although his cock had grown hard; he made no attempt to take off either his clothes or hers. Instead, he broke the kiss to smile down at her, one hand still cradling her neck, the other caressing the smoothness of her cheek. It was time he admitted his feelings to her.

"Adora, you know that I love you."

The smile she returned to him lit little stars in her eyes. "And I love you, David." Her hand brushed away stray hair that threatened to obscure his beautiful eyes.

"And Richard?"

"Yes, I love Richard, too. Just as you still love Lissa."

David leaned forward to kiss her alabaster forehead. "I only hope she and Richard find love as well."

* * * * *

Love was not what was on Lissa's mind as she waited among the "toys" of Richard's "playroom". She heard her husband say his goodbyes, and the sound of the car's ignition almost made her bolt. But then she grinned. Those two would make goo-goo eyes at each other most of the night. She sincerely hoped Richard had something much more exciting planned for her.

Richard made an effort to be quiet as he climbed the stairs to the room he had created for the woman of his dreams. Tonight would determine if Melissa was that woman. He had chosen his clothes with care tonight—black was suited for the fiendish designs he had upon Melissa's body and spirit. Dark loafers, pressed black slacks, a black belt with a plain silver buckle, and a black shirt worked to complete the image he wished to project.

Melissa had shown a great deal of promise the week before, and she had come back. Both promising signs. But he reserved his heart. Too many times he'd thought he had found a woman who could bear his passions; too many times he had been proven wrong. Adora was the woman he loved with his soul; was there a woman who could withstand the love of his body? Tonight he intended to push Lissa as far as he safely could. Only by discovering some of her limits would he know if she was worth any more of his time. He needed a woman strong enough to accept the dark thoughts he cherished in the depth of his heart, a woman strong enough to beg for her own sexual release. For Adora's sake, Richard hoped Melissa would prove capable.

Adora loved him, of that Richard was confident. Just as he was confident she knew how much he loved her in return. But a part of her he could not touch—the part that needed a gentler hand than his. After speaking with his wife, he was sure she had at least shown that side to David. Now if only the man's wife proved to be a competent slave.

The door to the room was open. Silently Richard leaned against the frame, a stern light in his eyes as he gazed upon the woman who would shortly give her body to him to use as his plaything. Lissa stood in the middle of the room, clasping her hands before her to dampen the urge to peek under the cloths of some of the more intriguing shapes. Richard allowed himself a small smile at her obedience.

Lissa jumped as Richard cleared his throat. She turned and found her breath catching again; framed against the doorway, the man she called Master embodied a fiend incarnate. His broad shoulders seemed to stretch the width of the opening, his head almost brushed the top. Curly black hair framed his dark face, and his sea-blue eyes smoldered with an as yet unexpressed passion. The goatee that surrounded his full lips gave his round face the illusion that he was a dangerous man. She resisted the urge to tug her skirt down so it would cover more of her legs. Instead, she placed her hands firmly at her sides and stood waiting.

Richard surveyed her, taking her measure. Lissa's choice in clothing for the night was not lost on him. Inside her was a slut seeking a safe outlet. Richard wasn't surprised. Many women he had met had similar yearnings. Trained by their upbringing to behave themselves, they nonetheless found themselves wanting to express a less-accepted behavior. Lissa's short skirt accentuated her long and shapely legs. If he could ever get her to wear such an outfit in public, every male would vie for her attention. Especially when those legs were accompanied by such a full bosom. The pink fabric across her breasts stretched to show their shape—her bra gave her a very nice cleavage. Oh, yes, she would certainly turn heads.

But such an event was in their future, not their present. The single, overhead light he had left on for her shone down with a most unflattering glare. The bare bulb filled the room with an intensity designed to make her uncomfortable. There was no soft light to hide behind. Richard wanted her to feel exposed. Remaining where he was, he gave her a command.

"Strip for me, slave."

Lissa's independent spirit flared only for a second before she dampened it. This was her choice, she reminded herself severely. Deliberately, her fingers unbuttoned her blouse, letting it fall open to reveal the pushup bra. She could not look him in the eye as embarrassment threatened to overwhelm her. Keeping her eyes down, she pushed the blouse off her shoulders letting it fall to her hands.

"Look at me, slave."

She did, not moving her head from its downcast position. *Eyes like saucers*, wasn't that how the phrase went? Richard noted her reaction, but did not waver.

"Fold it neatly and place it on the chair over here." Remaining in the doorway, he nodded to a straight-backed chair that sat to his right.

Lissa did so, becoming a bit more confident as she crossed the few steps that brought her closer to him. A whiff of his cologne tickled her nose. The clove scent was a powerful aphrodisiac and her stomach fluttered. Remaining in front of the chair and less than an arm's reach from him, her fingers moved to her waist to unfasten her skirt. But at a shake of his head, she stopped. Without moving from his comfortable spot against the doorframe, Richard crossed his arms over his expansive chest and nodded into the room.

"Back to the center of the room, slave. Undress there."

She understood. Cheeks burning now with her embarrassment, she walked back under the light in the center of the room and turned to face him again. The independent streak came to her aid and Lissa raised her chin almost defiantly as she undid the front closure on her bra instead of unbuttoning her skirt, letting her breasts hang free. He hadn't told her what to take off, only to undress.

When he nodded to the chair, she crossed the room, folding the bra as she came. Setting it on top of her folded shirt, she turned on her heel and once more took center stage.

But if he expected the skirt to fall next, she decided to make him wait. Slipping off her sandals, she bent to pick them up, keeping her legs straight and the view of her ass pointed away from him. With a challenge in her eye, she sauntered to the chair and placed the sandals beneath it before turning sharply again and returning to the center of the room.

Richard simply waited, letting her have her brief moment of triumph. In fact, her actions boded well. While carrying out his orders, she still managed to give them her own definite twist. Interesting.

Lissa's fingers undid the clasp of her skirt and she paused. Richard would now know she wore no panties at all. Not even a thong. Her cheeks burned anew as she let the skirt drop.

But Richard stopped her when she bent her knees to pick it up. "No, slave." He did not move, but the firm, commanding tone in his voice made her stop to listen. "You will retrieve it the same way you picked up your sandals. But you will face the opposite direction."

Lissa's eyes narrowed in humiliation. How dare he? She turned around and bent over, giving him a full view of her ass and pussy lips as she did so. Damn him for besting her. She stalked over and dropped the skirt on top of the pile.

One look from him, however, and she knew his meaning. He might be amused, but his direction was clear — he wanted her back under that horrid light.

She went. Totally naked, she stood in the center of the room, not even a soft light to hide her imperfections. The dark mole on her right breast marred the translucent peach of that full globe. The scar on her side from a childhood appendectomy screamed a pink color. And a small, round white spot of skin, her birthmark, gleamed palely on her left side in the bright incandescent light.

All the time he watched Lissa undress, Richard remained casually leaning against the doorway. Her humiliation at stripping naked for him tightened the coil in his belly — a coil he would continue to wind until the feelings of sexual release became too strong to ignore. Stepping toward her on silent feet, Richard continued her humiliation. "Put your hands up behind your head, slave. Clasp your fingers together."

Lissa did as she was told, her breasts rising as she did so. Richard meandered around her, taking his time with his examination and noting her small blemishes. The beauty mark on her breast, the light pink line of a former pain, birthmark that denoted her individuality. Each one marking her as a unique and beautiful woman.

Lissa, determined not to squirm under his inspection, stood still, the muscles in her legs tight with anticipation and embarrassment. With no way to hide her imperfections, she felt vulnerable. What if he found something that repulsed him? As his examination continued, she grew damp and there was absolutely no way she could hide it. He commanded her; she wanted him to take complete control.

"Tell me what you are thinking, my slave."

He stood behind her; she dared not turn around to answer him. She opened her mouth to speak, shut it, and opened it again.

"I am thinking that I want to be mad at you for how you speak to me. It's demeaning and rude. But there's something about you calling me "slave" that just makes my knees want to turn to jelly. I don't understand how I can feel both at the same time, but I do."

"Do you want to submit to me?"

"Yes!"

"Do you want to submit to just anyone? Or only to me?"

Richard came around in front of her. She still gripped her hands behind her head, but Lissa's face was alive with her struggle to understand her own feelings.

"Only to you. Definitely. I could never do this with anyone else."

"Why not?"

"Because you...well, you..." She stopped, stumped. Just why would she only do this for him? Because his tanned skin, dark goatee and vivid blue eyes gave him the look of a handsome devil come to claim her soul? Because her own husband had taken a fancy to his wife? Or was it something deeper?

"Say it, Melissa. I wish to hear the answer from your lips."

He knew he was pushing her. But it wasn't only his ego that wanted to hear the answer. He wanted to know how close he was to touching the wild animal inside her.

"I can only do this with you because you've made me comfortable doing this with you." When he said nothing, only raised a dark, sexy eyebrow at her, she continued. "You're patient with me. In spite of some of the words you use with me, I think that, deep down inside, you respect me. As a person. I could not do this at all with someone who just wanted to tie me up and find a hole to stick his cock in."

Richard's booming laugh filled the room. That was not the answer he had expected, she'd given him one better.

"Put your arms down, Melissa." He waited until she had done so before standing before her, and tilting her head up so that she could read the truth in his eyes. "I do respect you; I'm glad you understand that. But I *do* intend to tie you up and, 'find a hole and stick my cock in' — tonight."

The twinkle in his eye told her meant it, and her pussy twitched in anticipation. His cock was huge, certainly larger than she had ever seen in real life before; even most of those she saw on the web paled in comparison. Remembering his size, her pussy contracted again. Could she take such a man without pain? Lissa smiled shyly at him. It was going to be fun finding out.

* * * * *

Adora lay entwined in David's arms, his leg thrown over her thighs, his semi-erect cock nestled in the hollow of her hip. Almost lazily they had undressed and now cuddled together, needing only a sheet over them in the warm summer night. The candles cast their romantic spell over the room and Adora sighed.

"Was that a sigh of discontent?" David pulled his head back and peered down at the beautiful woman in his arms.

"The opposite." Adora's sultry voice, smooth as velvet in the night, caressed his ear. "I cannot believe how at home I feel in your arms. How protected."

"But you feel protected in Richard's arms as well."

"It is a different kind of protection. Richard would fight for me. He would kill any man who tried to hurt me. He protects my body; you protect my soul."

David wasn't sure what to say. She was right; David was a poor warrior when it came to a physical battle. But hurt kittens and wounded psyches he could deal with.

"Does that mean you don't want to dominate me?" He couldn't resist teasing, but Adora answered him seriously.

"I dominate men because of my need for revenge." She turned her head so she could look at him. His blond hair, tinged with the soft yellows of the light, brought out the almost white highlights, making it look as if he wore a halo around his head. No knight in shining armor for her; that image belonged to Richard. No, David was her angel, come to her from the very heart of Heaven to save her.

His cock stirred and she smiled. And a very sexy angel at that.

"I don't need to dominate you, David, because you treat me as an equal."

He knew what she meant. In the past men either tried to control her, or she controlled the men; she knew no other way. Even with Richard, who loved her with all of his heart, in the bedroom, equality was not an option. But David never wanted it any other way.

Her blue eyes shone with unshed tears—not of submission or gratitude—but of utter contentment and peace. He brushed the backs of his knuckles along her soft cheek, trailing a finger to trace the sharp line of her jaw. Leaning forward, he pulled her toward him as their lips met in a tender kiss.

Gently, like brushing one's lips over a rose petal, their lips caressed. Their breaths, begun separately, mingled, becoming one in the closeness of their kiss. And when their kiss deepened, their bodies moved to join.

Adora's legs parted; David's cock grew hard. But still he lingered at her lips, her taste heady like a rare, sweet wine; he wished to drink his fill. And when he had, he turned to the sweetness of her skin, blazing a trail of his kisses down her neck to the little hollow between her collarbones. His tongue eagerly explored that sweet spot.

Adora's head fell back as she enjoyed his explorations. The hard muscles of his back rippled under her fingers as his hand cupped her breast, and his mouth moved down to enclose the nipple. She whimpered and dug her nails into the skin of his back, urging him onward.

His mouth enjoyed the sweet taste of her nipple too much to leave just yet, however. Instead, he rested his body on hers, the warmth of her pussy pressing against the smooth skin of his chest. When her legs encircled his back, he snuggled in, comfortable with her breast for his pillow.

* * * * *

Stretched fully on the piece of furniture Richard had referred to as a bed, Lissa decided her first name for it was the better one. A rack.

Instructed to lie face up on the wooden platform, Lissa now lay bound to it. Not only her wrists were encased in the wide leather cuffs, this time Richard cuffed her ankles as well, then spread her body and tied her arms and legs to the four corners of the platform.

But she was still not spread enough for him. He certainly had a good view of her arousal; white cream already appeared among the dark hairs surrounding the slit he would soon penetrate. Tight as he had bound her, there was still too much wiggle room. He wanted her immobile for what he intended.

And so he bound her further, taking white cotton rope and securing her legs both above and below the knee to spread them wide. Anchoring her waist to the eyehooks on the side of the table, he tied her arms taut above her head, on both sides of her elbows, effectively immobilizing her. When he was done, he surveyed his work.

The one overhead light still cast its unflattering glare. Richard turned it off, plunging the room into momentary darkness. No light filtered in from anywhere. Lissa tried to squirm on the bed as her thoughts got the better of her. What was he doing? What was *she* doing? Letting him tie her so thoroughly that all she could do was tighten and relax muscles. All she had control over was her head, and that she could only move from side to side as well as raise a half inch or so. Richard's bindings were secure. In the darkness, she heard his seductive baritone.

"I intend to flog you tonight, Melissa. To have you feel the caress of the leather across your virgin flesh. I wish to hear your screams sing into the night."

Her pussy flooded as his words careened through her mind, setting her passion on fire. But she did not cry out to stop him, not even as she felt the leather thongs brushing softly against her breasts.

That whimpering sound in the back of her throat caused Richard to smile. Knowing her mind reeled with her helplessness, he let the moment linger, slowly dragging his chosen flogger along the twin hills of her breasts and down along the flat plane of her stomach.

The darkness served to heighten her anticipation; he let the anticipation build. One heartbeat. A second. Another dozen heartbeats in the night before he stepped away to add light to the equation. Let her see the instrument of her torment.

A soft, incandescent light flared over near the door, a welcome light. Lissa lifted her head, but could not see the small lamp. She could, however, clearly see what her Master held.

Short, flat thongs of light brown suede, as long as her forearm, hung from the handle in his hand. As she watched, he came back to her, holding it up for her inspection. The brown handle contained the ends of all the thongs woven together into a solid grip of leather. No chance one would snap out; this flogger had been made by a master craftsman. Three parts of her brain held separate reactions to the sight. The most objective part of her brain registered the beauty and workmanship of such a magnificent object, while another part of her mind recoiled at the thought of those thongs biting into her skin, yet a third part sent signals of arousal to her pussy, which promptly throbbed with the desire to experience the sharp caress of the leather.

"Sing for me slave. I wish to hear your sounds."

Richard snapped the flogger with no further warning to land directly across her vulnerable breasts. Lissa gasped in surprise. The muscles of her body tensed in their bindings, but she could not avoid the second lash of those stinging leather thongs.

"Sing for me, Melissa! I wish to hear your voice."

The flogger landed again and Lissa's natural quietness gave way to her desire to sing for her Master. She wanted him to stop; she wanted him to continue forever. The sounds bubbled up inside; the flogger landed, and her tightened muscles forced the cries from her.

In the soft light, Richard watched the helpless woman thrash against her bindings. Caught in a net of his own weaving, she could not escape his torment. He listened to her cries and reveled in the sound of her pleasure as he slapped the leather thongs against her skin.

Richard changed his tempo; the lashes fell more slowly, but harder each time. Her cries became grunts as her face winced in pain. A pain he knew aroused her as it sent the endorphins coursing through her body and took her to new heights.

She endured the blows that rained along her breasts, closing her eyes to savor the sweet pain and enjoy the rising tension building in her body, her lower lips now soaked with her need. The outside world floated away; all that remained was the will of her Master, and the touch of the leather.

Again Richard changed his tactics as her body quieted under the lash and her cries turned to soft whimpers. Her breasts flushed a bright pink; the nipples, hard as stones, stood erect. Richard smiled; he had plans for those nipples later.

* * * * *

The scent of Adora's sex drifted up to David where his head rested on her breast, tempting him, stirring the latent passions inside. Dipping a finger down to rub against her lips, he liked the soft murmur his touch produced. Almost lazily, he brought his wet fingers to his mouth and sucked them clean. Her sudden intake of breath made him smile.

"I like how you taste, Adora. A little salty, perhaps, but actually quite nice."

"Oh, David, taste me again?" She wiggled a little underneath him, inviting him with more than just words.

"Of course." He grinned and reached down again, this time stopping a moment to flick her clit with his finger, eliciting some marvelous whimpers and a little more wiggling.

"Is someone getting needy?" he teased as he scooped his finger through her slit and raised it to his lips again.

For answer, Adora only grinned and waggled her hips under his chest.

Poised, ready to lick his fingers, David changed his mind. Instead, he leaned forward, inching up the bed to place a wet finger on Adora's mouth. She parted her lips to accept his gift to her, but he shook his head and she closed her mouth, her brow furrowed in puzzlement.

"Let me paint your lips with the scent of your pussy; I want us to share your taste when I kiss you next."

She smiled and let him trace a line of wetness over her lips, and when he bent his head to take his kiss, she tilted her head up, enjoying the salty taste of her arousal.

David felt her hand slip around behind his head, pulling him deeper into the kiss. Surrounded by Adora's presence in her scent, her touch, the warmth of her skin, his cock hardened.

She felt his erection poke her hip. His arousal mirrored her own. Her lips parted, inviting his tongue in to explore the inner softness of her mouth. David obliged her. Slowly at first, then increasing in tempo, their tongues caressed each other. Both moaned as David's cock pressed harder against her skin. The maroon head, swollen with his need, raised itself proudly in the candlelit night.

Moving as one, Adora spread her legs as David slipped between them. He could not take his eyes from her beauty, the desire to sink his cock past her luscious mound overwhelming him. Her golden hair spread on the pillows like the halo of an angel. Her eyes, two sapphire windows to her soul and dark with passion, urged him on.

And still he savored the moment, enjoying the sight of her nipples, hard little round nubs that had tasted of sweetness on his tongue, and her pert breasts, now flattened as she lay on her back, their roundness bouncing from side to side as she wiggled her hips upward, begging with her body for his entrance.

He leaned down to capture her mouth, pulling on her full lips, each one in turn. And only then, when he held her mouth captive in his embrace, did he push his cock against her opening...slowly...deliberately...forcing himself inside.

She moaned under him and tried to move her head, but he held her in his kiss. Her lips parted and she let his tongue penetrate her mouth as his cock penetrated her pussy. Deeper and deeper he pushed, harder and harder she pushed up against him, willing him in, wanting to feel herself surrounded by his love and his body.

Their bodies rocked as one. David thrusting deep into her tight, warm pussy, Adora's legs wrapped around him, pushing him into the secrets of her soul. David's groans sang counterpoint to Adora's cries—a crescendo in the night—two souls yearning for release.

They came together. Adora's eyes shining blue beacons of trust, desire, and love as David's shone with protection, caring, and love. Their souls touched—naked to each other—and David loved Adora for what she shared.

* * * * *

Richard's slave floated in a haze of his creation, willing to float or come as he commanded. He switched the flogger for a different device; this one a wand of flexible plastic wrapped in a wide black leather sheath. The flat end, about two inches wide and shaped like a small hand, slapped against Lissa's pussy lips when Richard snapped the crop against her most sensitive area.

Lissa jumped more in shock than pain. Suspended in her flogger-induced haze, Richard's pause as he switched instruments gave her time to enjoy the heat the leather had spread over her skin. Warm and tingling with little fires, her chest rose and fell with each deep breath she took. The slap of the new toy brought her out of her reverie, making her concentrate on the kindling of a new fire between her legs.

The dark brown hair of her mound gave scant protection to the blows that now warmed her skin. Never landing in the same place twice, Richard kept her off balance. A blow to her inner thigh left an imprint of the little hand. A matching blow to the inside of her other thigh gave her twin spots of pink.

And now he set up a quick tattoo. Quickly slapping the end of the crop from side to side, he reddened the skin between her legs, listening as her cries increased. "Yes, slave. Let me hear your voice."

Lissa screamed as the crop's tempo continued. Her head tossed from side to side, her eyes opened but did not focus. The stinging drove her mad. She cried out to him in wordless pleas, language had left her. The unbearable tension built until even her screams brought no relief.

Richard's cock grew hard as the intensity of the woman's screams increased, the animal inside him raged to throw away the crop and ravage her there on the table.

With an oath, he let the animal loose. Later he would look for the crop, he didn't care where it had landed. He wanted more. Grabbing her reddened thighs with his hands, he rubbed the skin, pushing the heat into her body, his touch agony. She screamed again as her pussy pooled its white cream on the table in her need.

He could contain himself no longer. Unzipping his pants and not bothering to take them off, he mounted the sturdy table, his magnificent cock dark with his desire, framed by the dark clothing he wore.

Lissa's pussy opened in her need, anticipating, wanting to be split by his thickness. Yet her mind cried in fear, straining against the bindings to close her legs and keep him out.

Her cries fueled Richard's lust. The woman uttered no safeword that would force him to cage the animal. He gave it free rein, poising the purple tip of his cock at the edge of her sopping pussy, the sides of his legs scraping the reddened skin of her whipped thighs.

"Beg me, slave."

Lissa's cry echoed through the room, but no words formed.

"Beg me!"

The raw power in his voice brought her mind to bear. Straining against the ropes to push her pussy toward him, she pleaded. "Take me, please, oh, God, please!"

"What do you want, slave? Tell me!"

The humiliation of having to beg, coupled with the fire in her tender skin and her total helplessness broke the last reserve of will Lissa had. The untouchable wildness of her spirit cried out to the dominating ferocity of his. Screaming, she begged him. "Take me! Let me feel your cock inside me! Please!"

Her cry ended on a scream as Richard thrust into her, slamming his cock in almost half its length in one push. Stretched muscles felt ripped open as her pussy clenched against the intruder, before opening again to invite him deeper.

He felt the invitation and took advantage of it, pulling out to thrust in again.

"Open your eyes slave, and give me your climax. Come for me, slut."

He saw the animal in her dark eyes; the independent, calm and quiet woman vanished into the night. With a snarl, her brows furrowed as he commanded her; and then she gasped as her body tensed. Richard saw her nostrils flaring as she hovered there, then listened to her screams as she plunged off the cliff, her body writhing against the ropes as she came over and over.

Savagely, he thrust his cock into her, letting his own need drive him now. His cries in the night, feral and untamed, joined hers as he pumped his seed deep inside her. His body pounded her unmercifully as he took what he needed from his slave. Groaning, he emptied himself and hung upon the edge of sanity until he could no longer hold his body off her with his arms. Exhausted, he collapsed upon the twin cushions of her breast and listened to the wild beating of her heart.

* * * * *

The second-to-last candle guttered and went out. Only one dim flame still lit the room as David and Adora rested in each other's arms. Neither spoke. Words between them would be trite. So entwined, they fell asleep at peace with the world.

* * * * *

It took an effort of will on Richard's part to untie Lissa from her bindings. He had little strength left. Once her hands were free and she could sit up, she helped by undoing the bindings around her legs as Richard coiled and stowed the several pieces of rope. The leather cuffs remained locked in place, however, as Richard led her to the bedroom. Gently he covered her body with a light sheet as he lay down beside her, his fingers tracing the red lines of the ropes, his cool hands soothing the heat of her skin.

"Tell me what you are thinking, Melissa."

His voice was soft, reserved. Almost as if he were afraid she would run away in the morning. She turned to face him, the cuffs jingling as she did so.

"Permission to touch you, Sir?"

Apprehension stirred in his gut, he gave permission anyway. "Yes, you have permission."

He leaned on one arm before her, his face above hers in the soft bedroom light. Softly she caressed his cheek with the backs of her fingers, tracing the line of his goatee, no hint of the devil in his face. She caught only a faint glimpse of his vulnerability before his eyes grew stern again; the ever-present Master of her being. Gently Lissa leaned forward to brush a kiss upon his lips. And when he did not pull away, she let the kiss deepen, her lips parting, their breaths shared as Lissa held her Master in her arms and calmed the wild animal. Her heart moved with pity for the man. To have had no outlet for such a great passion must have been a hardship indeed. But she was here now, and would see that his animal had a home.

And when the kiss ended, she answered him. "That is what I am thinking, dear Sir."

Chapter 7

Outside the window, the night paled as pink lace and purple ribbons of cloud spread across the sky. The sparrow began his merry song; a cardinal whistled a greeting to his mate. And in the dim light growing in the bedroom, David gazed upon the sleeping form of the beautiful woman in his arms.

The rose light peeked around the edges of the shades to fall on her face, brushing her cheeks with romantic color. A stray strand of gold had fallen across her eyes in the night; David lifted the flaxen lock and kissed it before carefully placing the soft wisp on the pillow.

Adora stirred, so David slipped out of bed, careful to not disturb her slumber. The bathroom was just around the corner. He decided to take his shower and let her sleep a bit longer.

Turning the water on, his mind turned over the sex of the night before. He had intended to get Adora to speak more of her past, but that hadn't happened. Their mutual desires had gotten the better of them and they'd spent the evening exploring each other's bodies instead of their pasts. Not that David had much of a past worth spending time on.

The hot water cascaded down the muscles of his back and David lathered his chest as he considered the relationship between Adora and Richard. They were very much in love; there was no doubt about that. Just as he and Lissa were joined forever. Could he help Adora get what she needed from Richard? And more importantly, did he want her to?

He rinsed the soap from his chest as he struggled with the reality of his love for her. If Richard gave her vanilla sex, then of what use was David? And did he only love her for the sex?

Questions piled up in his mind as he washed his short, sandy hair, ducking under the water to rinse. Suddenly he realized he was not alone.

Pulling himself out of the stream of hot water, he shook his head so he could open his eyes. But Adora's giggle gave away her position before he needed to look. She stood just outside the shower, her head peeking in through the curtain at the very nice view he provided.

Even soaking wet, David was an attractive man. The strong cheekbones of his clean-shaven face accentuated a strong chin and a smile that tended to be shyly sexy. Naked in the shower, with water running over his muscles, Adora could see the physical strength usually hidden by his white shirts. And although his cock was not hard at the moment; she knew the tender power that lay quietly between his muscular thighs.

"May I join you?" Adora's normally soft voice shouted over the noise of the shower.

David made a welcoming gesture and pulled the curtain back, holding out his hand to steady her as first one slender leg and then the other stepped over the side and into the tub before him. Ignoring the water, he pulled her into his arms and gave her a soft, good-morning kiss.

"Here, let me wash your back for you," Adora instructed when they parted.

Obediently, David turned around for her and let her soap his back. First running the bar of soap over his skin, Adora's long fingers then worked it into a lather as she massaged his back at the same time. Convinced she had covered every inch, David remained still as her fingers continued to dig into his muscles, turning him into a standing pile of Jell-O.

"All right. Rinse!"

He turned toward her again, letting the last of the soap rinse away. "Your turn!"

David made a mental note to talk to Lissa about putting on an addition with a large shower. A *very* large shower. Their normal-sized tub in their fairly small bathroom did not afford Adora and him much room to move about. Changing positions with her would have been easier if he had gotten out of the tub at one end and back in at the other. Still, with much giggling and laughing, Adora squeezed past David and he managed to not fall out of the tub in the process.

Facing her, David watched as she leaned back into the water flow to soak her hair, the warm water cascading over her face and skipping to her pert breasts before plunging to the tub's porcelain floor. Leaning down, he pulled her nipple into his mouth, sucking the water off as it careened from the tip. He felt the nipple grow hard in his mouth.

Taking up the soap, he rubbed the front of her body with the small bar, being sure to cover every square inch he could reach. Adora wasn't much shorter than he was, so he could cover all of her upper body without trouble. Before he went below her waist, however, he gestured for her to turn around and rinse the slippery lather from her front.

With a smile, she did so and his hands encircled her, rubbing her stomach and breasts free of all the soap. She leaned back and rested her head on his shoulder, simply enjoying the touch of his hands on her wet skin. When those hands picked up the soap again and dipped down to slide the bar between her legs, she willingly spread her limbs wide and gave him permission

Sliding the soap bar along her slit, he felt her body tense in his arms. When her arms stretched up and reached behind her to caress his hair, David took that as an open invitation to explore deeper. Turning the bar on its end, he slid it from her clit towards her ass. When it sank deep into her pussy and she gasped, he grinned, his cock responding to her obvious arousal.

Putting his left arm around her chest, he held her firmly so that she would not fall as he fucked her pussy with a bar of soap. He pushed it in deep, then waited for her body to expel the slippery oval. Not letting it fall, he pushed it in again, over and over as she whimpered her need.

"Oh, yes, David. Make me come. Please?" Her voice, almost drowned in the noise of the water, pleaded with him.

"Then come for me, Adora. Let me feel you."

David pushed his thumb against her clit, rubbing it in circles as he increased the tempo of the soap. He felt the muscles of her body tense and her fingers, entwined in his hair, flexed and pulled his head down to her shoulder as her body responded. A shudder shook her entire being and she gasped, holding her breath as a second shudder built and released. A third pulse came and David held onto her as she let her body be consumed by her orgasm.

With a final shudder, she opened her eyes. David let the soap fall into his hand and she gave a little shake as if warding off a chill. Letting go of him, she turned to face the man who gave her such powerful orgasms armed with nothing other than a shower and a bar of soap.

* * * * *

The birdsong seeped into Lissa's consciousness; she breathed deep, inhaling the fresh air coming in the open window as she stretched to meet the morning. But her arms pulled up short, interrupting her stretch. In confusion, she opened her eyes and examined her surroundings.

The last thing she remembered was falling asleep in a soft bed with Richard's head nestled on her breasts, his arms encircling her in a protective embrace. His side of the bed was empty now and Lissa realized the shower was on.

Again she tried moving; her hands lay beside her head, the black cuffs still locked on with their golden locks, but an addition caused her breath to catch. The cuffs were locked together; a thick silver chain ran from them to somewhere over her head. Pulling on the chain produced no downward movement; already taut, her arms could go no further.

Bending her head back, Lissa could see the chain attached to an eyebolt in the side of the headboard. No lock held it in place; the last link of the chain looped through the steel hole; a permanent fastening. She had not noticed it before because...well...because her mind had been on other matters.

Rolling onto her back, she raised her arms and discovered that allowed her some movement. She could go up with her hands, but not down further than her face. Resting her hands on top of her head, she turned her attention to her legs.

These, too, were still bound in the black leather cuffs. Like her wrists, her ankles were locked together; a chain ran from the lock to a matching eyehook in the side of the footboard. Experimenting, she scooched herself down the bed until her arms were extended and her knees bent. In this position, she could open her knees, but not far. Her cuffed ankles prevented that from happening.

The sound of the water ceased and Lissa pushed herself up the bed again. Any sheet that had covered her in the warm night had long since balled into a heap and now it pushed against the small of her back, making her decidedly uncomfortable. Without thinking, she lowered her hand to pull it out from under her; the chain brought her movement up short and she was left to wiggle on the bed, trying to dislodge the offending cloth.

"That's a nice view to come in to." Richard's low baritone drawled from the doorway.

Immediately Lissa stopped her squirming. "Good morning. The sheet is under me." She expected he would come over and remove it, making her comfortable once more.

"Is it?" Richard ignored her predicament, going over to the dresser at the foot of the bed to comb his wet, tousled hair. Only a towel covered him, the ends neatly and securely tucked in at his waist. The deep blue of the towel brought her attention to the blue of his eyes; she watched his reflection in the mirror. He paid her no mind at all.

Damn him. He didn't want to help her; she wasn't going to ask again. Lissa squirmed a bit more but only succeeded in making a bigger bulge of sheet under her. In an attempt to get comfortable, she tried lying on her side, but with her hands and feet bound, she could not get her elbow under her for leverage.

Her unbound hair fell across her face and she batted at it with her bound hands. If there was one thing she hated, it was hair in her face. But her angle was wrong and waves of brown fell back across her eyes. She tossed her head to get rid of the offending stuff, but still she could not see. Half on her side, half on her back, she had worked herself into quite a predicament.

Richard watched her in the mirror when she started her struggles anew. He knew what she wanted from him, but if she were truly to be his slave, there were some things she needed to learn. Number one was that he was the Master and she the slave.

He saw her hair slide down off her shoulder and across her eyes and remembered the feel of it in his hands. Last night he'd spent quite a bit of time running his hands through her thick tresses, enjoying the silkiness as it passed through his fingers. Now it lay in tangles and her efforts to dislodge the hair from her face were unsuccessful. He would wait a bit longer; would she come to him on her own?

After several minutes she stilled, her body awkwardly placed on the bed. Richard watched as she crept closer to the edge of the bed, ready to stop her if she came too near; he didn't want her to fall. But she would learn how to address him. And she would learn her place.

Richard knew what he was asking. The woman was not his wife; he did not want her to be. Adora was the perfect partner for him in every way but in her sexual submission. That was the rub, and that was why Lissa now lay bound to his bed in chains. In their several meetings, Lissa had shown a willingness to submit to his whims, but Richard sensed she always held something back. Only at the moment of purest ecstasy did she allow him a glimpse. The time had come to put her to the ultimate test. Was she willing to submit *every* part of her to him even when they weren't having sex?

Richard had decided that he wished to totally own this woman. Every part of her for the length of time she was his. He wanted a complete surrender from Lissa. Not just a sex slave in the Hollywood sense, but a true servant, a woman who submerged her own sense of self into his, melding with him and becoming one with him. A woman who found her fulfillment in the realization of his desires and wishes.

And then went back to her own husband when he was finished with her.

There was a certain selfishness to his desires. Richard accepted that. But then, Lissa had said the same thing about her own needs. She had mentioned that she felt she was only taking, and not giving when he played with her, not realizing she'd given him the greatest gift of all — herself.

So now he waited. She lay panting on the bed, the most recent attempt to remove the hair from her face again fruitless. Would she ask him? And how would she phrase her request?

Lissa knew Richard was still in the room despite the fact that her hair prevented her from seeing a darn thing. And she was relatively sure he watched her trying to get her hair off her face. Her arms grew tired from trying to flip herself over and she finally stopped trying. Why didn't he help her? How more obvious could she be while chained up this way?

Of course, if she had just remained still in the beginning and not played around, experimenting with her bindings, she wouldn't be in this predicament now. The sheet was the least of her worries. The edge of the bed was near, she could feel it under her elbow. And her hair gave her a claustrophobic feeling she didn't like at all.

A faint noise from the bottom of the bed reassured her that he was still in the room. "Master?" Her voice was tremulous as she fought anger and frustration and helplessness. What did he want from her and why didn't he help her?

"Yes, slave?" Richard kept his voice neutral. His natural instincts were to let her out of this situation; yet he knew if he wanted her trained to his ways, he needed to be firm.

"Would you please help me?"

"Help you do what, slave?" He was not about to make it easy for her.

She thought for a moment. What did she want? Out of her bindings? No. He was right to make her be more specific.

"Master, would you take my hair from my face? Please?" One thing at a time, she decided. Once she saw his face, she would know how to proceed. If this was just a power trip thing...

His elegant fingers lifted the locks of hair from where they hid her beautiful brown eyes and he gently brushed the remaining stray hairs till all was tucked away.

Stooping down so he could see her face in the morning light, he cocked his head and smiled at her.

Lissa grinned back. No power trip. He only wanted obedience. That she could give him easily. "Is it your will I lie uncomfortably? If it is, then I shall lie on a bed of nails for you, Sir."

Richard laughed. He loved this woman for the way she continually surprised him. "It is my will you speak to me with a proper tone and with proper manners." He brushed the backs of his knuckles across her cheek, still creased with sleep. His eyes grew serious. "It is also my will that you stay as I placed you."

She heard the admonition, but could not give in just yet. "Then am I not to play with my bindings? To see what I can and cannot do?"

"You may, of course. But I do not expect complaints if your wiggling gets you into a situation that makes you uncomfortable. In fact, I do not expect complaints at all."

His tone, gentle but firm, brooked no argument. She gave him none, simply nodding. "I understand."

His raised eyebrow gave him that devilish air again and she grinned as she added his title, "Master."

"Is there anything else you wish, slave?"

She smiled at him, but he could read the unease in her eyes. "Sir, I have to go to the bathroom." Such an admission colored her cheeks. When he did not change his expression, she understood she needed to ask for permission. Could she? Could she subjugate herself to such a degree? The pressure on her bladder answered for her.

"Please, Master, will you unchain me so that I may use the bathroom?"

He saw the increasing desperation in her eyes. Need drove her this time, but they had made strides. All right, maybe only baby steps, not strides. He was patient.

Reaching toward her, he unlocked her wrists from the chain, then her ankles. She needed no help to stand. In seconds she was out of the room, and he heard the bathroom door close. Time to push another limit.

She didn't intend to dally. Lissa took care of her needs and flushed the toilet, standing before the large mirror over the sink as she washed her hands. The body reflected there, however, caught and held her attention. She found herself twisting and turning, examining every red line, every pink flush that marked her skin.

Only after a full minute of inspection did she realize most of the lines were sleep lines. The pink spots, however, were definitely marks placed there by the hand of her Master. The thought caused a freshening of her arousal and she hurriedly wiped it away in embarrassment.

Richard stepped into the hallway and eyed the still-closed door, frowning in concern. Had he pushed her too far this morning? Was she having second thoughts? Or was she ill? The second flush of the toilet only added to his fears.

But the door opened and she stood there, radiant in the morning light, her nudity glowing with her arousal. Her heavy breasts, still slightly pink from the flogger, swung seductively as she slowly crossed to him. The scent of her arousal wafted up and mingled with the perfume of the soap she had used to wash her face and hands. Stopping before him, he could see the flutter of her heartbeat in the hollow of her throat. Strong, steady, its quick beat indicating her excitement.

"Kneel."

A one-word command that brooked no disobedience. She knelt in the hallway, her eyes falling to his towel-clad waist. The thick hair of his chest tapered here, pointing like an arrow to that which still lay hidden by the soft terrycloth. Try as she might, she could not contain the small smile that danced in her eyes and on her face.

* * * * *

David never realized drying a woman's body could be so much fun. Although Adora had wrapped her hair up in a towel that wound around her head like a turban, the rest of her body dripped in some of the most intriguing places. He caught a drop of water just as it was about to leave the warm cavity of her golden pussy, letting it fall onto his tongue as she giggled above him. Toweling dry her long, slender legs, he knelt before her, enjoying the view, and the drips.

"Bend your knees a bit...perfect!" He leaned forward to lick a second drip that stubbornly clung to her pussy lips. Lightly brushing his tongue against her skin, he skillfully flicked the tiny drop into his mouth. Although no trace of creamy whiteness showed, David knew Adora was aroused; her wonderfully musky scent hung in the tight space like a bouquet of flowers in a small room. He inhaled deeply before plunging his nose deep into her slit to nuzzle her pussy.

"David!" Adora's startled cry and grab for the sink betrayed her sudden arousal rather than shock at his actions. That and the fact that his nose now bore the evidence.

He pulled back and grinned up at her. "Yes, my dear? Is there a problem?"

She laughed and swatted him playfully with the towel she was using to return his favor, drying his back as he dried her legs. "No problem. I'm just hoping to get my turn at *you*, that's all." Waggling her eyebrows at him so he would catch her meaning, she glanced down to where his cock was hidden from her to drive home her point.

"Ah, yes. Well, I do need to be dried off. You're right there." He stood and his cock came into the light, fully erect and still damp from the shower. Glimmering in the morning sun, the smooth pink tip invited Adora's attentions. She pushed him back so that he leaned against the sink, then knelt before him on the towel she had used to dry him. Soft downy hairs covered him, creating a golden halo around his glistening cock.

The warmth of her mouth encircled him and David's entire body relaxed into her embrace. She glanced up at him; their eyes met and twinkled in sheer enjoyment of each other's company.

Neither of them hurried this morning, neither wanted to rush. Adora's attention to his cock was studied, she examined every centimeter with the tip of her tongue. Exploring and discovering the secret spaces behind the bulging tip, reveling in the velvety softness of the underside, finally she licked the salty pre-cum from the tiny slit, a mirror to her own pussy now throbbing again with need.

David's hand on her head stopped her explorations. Glancing up, she saw the passion in his eyes; he held out his hand to her and she placed her slender fingers into his open palm. Lifting her up, David led her out of the bath and back toward the sunlit bedroom.

* * * * *

Kneeling in the hallway with Richard towering over her, looking once more like a nefarious Gypsy king, Lissa's body trembled with anticipation. Sunlight poured out of the open bedroom door and bathed him in a fiery light while she knelt in shadow. His dark hair, still wet from his shower and slicked back from his face, accentuated the high angles of his cheekbones; the sun gave him a ruddy glow. His full and sensuous lips curled in a snarl; the contained passion in his eyes made her heart leap.

Richard saw the quickening of her breath and the sudden fear in her eyes and smiled. It was not a smile of kindness. His eyes narrowed as he looked down on her; the growl in his voice was not feigned. "What are you thinking, slave?"

Her answer was immediate. "Sometimes you scare me, although I know you won't hurt me. But you get a look in your eye and it sends a shiver through me." A shiver ran along her spine even as she said the words and she smiled shyly up at him. "But if I wanted to run away, I'd use the safeword, and I do not choose to use it at this time."

Richard turned on his heel and walked down the hall, past the bedroom door, stopping at another door further along. He paused before it, then barked another one word instruction. "Come."

Deep in her soul it rankled at being treated in such a manner. She barely acknowledged its existence. Putting her hands on the floor in front of her, she crawled along the hall, past the door to the bedroom, not so much like a dog called to heel, but more like a cat stalking its prey. Desire glowed in her eyes. She wanted his commands. She demanded them from him.

Lissa knew exactly which door he stood in front of; the dark walls of the playroom beckoned. With a single nod of his head, Richard instructed her to enter and watched as she went in on all fours. It had not been his intent to have her crawl down the corridor, but when she did, his heartbeat quickened at the feral look in her eye and his body responded. If Lissa noticed the bulge under his towel, she gave no sign.

"Onto the bed."

Richard referred to the rack. Lissa crawled up onto the platform, the locks on her cuffs jingling as she did so. Behind her, Richard pulled up a shade and sunlight streamed into the room.

"Stay on you hands and knees, slave."

Silently Richard locked her ankles into the eyehooks at the edge of the rack, spreading her knees to make her pussy more available. He left the room, returning a moment later with a towel from the bath. This he folded and set down on the wooden surface just under Lissa. He motioned her to put her head down on it; laying a cheek on the soft terrycloth, she put herself into the most vulnerable position she had been in so far.

On her knees, with her head down this way, her ass stuck up straight into the air. Her bound ankles prevented her from closing her legs. Only her hands remained free.

Richard's cock throbbed painfully, but he was not yet finished. Taking a small length of twine, he took up first one of her cuffed wrists, then the other, slipping the thin rope through the loops and tying them together behind her back. Now all her weight was on her knees, and her cheek.

"You have a beautiful pussy for me to torment, my dear. Did you know that?"

Richard stood back and admired the perfect view he now had of her body. Her pussy lips, already swelling with desire, puffed between her legs. Between those folds, her clit lay hidden, waiting for his attention. But above that glorious slit, lay another area of pink tenderness, an area still virgin if he was not mistaken.

Lissa could not answer in this position. She also could not see what he was doing and that made her throat swell with fear and excitement. Would he use the flogger on her again? She eyed the far wall where the toys hung in neat order. Or something stronger? A thin line of her juices squeezed out of her pussy to drip onto the wood beneath her.

* * * * *

They lingered at each other's lips. Standing naked in the bedroom, David held Adora lightly in his arms; she enjoyed the feel of his damp hair in her fingers.

"I like kissing you." Adora's sultry voice murmured when David deviated from her mouth to kissing her neck.

He felt her weight relax into his hands as he left a new trail of wet kisses from the hollow of her throat up to the area behind her ear. He had not yet explored this spot.

With her hair still wrapped in the towel, however, David now had the perfect opportunity. He liked the way her breathing quickened and the little gasp she made when his breath tickled her ear.

"Kissing you is fast becoming one of my favorite pastimes," he whispered into that sexy ear, covered with terrycloth. Only a small part of the lobe showed and he turned his attention to it, kissing it and pulling it into his mouth for a small nibble. He liked those small gasps she made when he kissed a new part of her.

Adora's knees threatened to give way and she sagged deeper into David's embrace. The bed was beside them, David pulled away long enough to help her to sit, then sat beside her, covering her breast with one hand while returning to that spot behind her ear to kiss her again.

He felt Adora's hand on his thigh and his cock stiffened in response. Her fingers trailed little circular movements around and over his thighs, his balls, his belly. But never did they touch his now-throbbing cock. He teased her nipple with his fingers; she teased his cock by not touching it.

He endured the sweet torment for several minutes, exploring her neck, her cheeks, her lips. But soon the pain became unendurable.

"Let me inside you, Adora. Let me feel how warm and tight you are."

She answered him with her body, stretching out on the bed and spreading her legs in invitation as she pulled him to her. Soft mewling sounds came from the back of her throat, sounds of her building need.

Yet David still did not wish to rush. He knelt between her legs, pulling her body up to him, teasing them both with his cock just at the entrance to her pussy. Several times he pushed it just barely inside, only to pull it out again, enjoying the lingering tension and watching Adora's pert breasts rise with anticipation each time as she took in a deep breath, ready for his plunge.

But it was not so much a plunge as sliding home. David leaned forward, shifting his weight as he did so, and gathered her in his arms as his cock slid in.

He kissed her again, but not the soft kisses they'd exchanged earlier. Passion now had the two of them in hand and their tongues entwined even as their bodies moved to a dance only they could perform. The little noises in the back of Adora's throat intensified as her body urged him deeper, her legs bent around his back, pushing him on.

With a cry, Adora's muscles contracted around his cock, and David held back no longer. Groaning softly into her mouth, his seed emptied as all thought fled.

* * * * *

Richard saw her arousal, and his cock throbbed with his own need. The woman before him took all he dished out to her and gave him back more in return. Standing behind her, he slipped a finger possessively along the soaked line between her pussy lips.

"Little slave likes this position, I see."

"Yes," Lissa managed to gasp out. She tried to remain still, even though she wanted nothing more than to push back and skewer herself on his fingers. Richard had left her a generous amount of wiggle room, but she wasn't sure how much of it she really wanted.

Richard saw her struggle to not move. He had not given her such an order, yet it was clear she had anticipated his command. There was more to a Dominant/submissive relationship than just bondage. Lissa clearly understood that. It was easy to allow him to manipulate her when she was bound and could not move. Could she give him the same permissions when she was bound lightly? Did she have the discipline of mind?

"Do not move, Melissa. I control your body, you don't. Be still."

His fingers worked along her slit and her breath turned ragged from the effort. A cry escaped her lips as he flicked her clit several times, causing more and more wetness to form and drip silently over his hand. But she did not move.

A smile tugged at his lips; time to push her further. He let his wet fingers trail upward to her virgin ass. Pressing gently on her hole with his finger, he was rewarded by a small gasp.

Was he really going to do what she thought he was? Pressure built at her ass and she clenched it tight in defense.

"Relax your muscles, Melissa. It will only hurt if you fight me."

She heard the warning implicit in his tone. He intended to enter her ass, whether she relaxed or not. With an effort of will, she opened her cheek muscles to him.

His finger, wet with her own juices, slid in up to the first knuckle. The feeling wasn't unpleasant at all. In fact, her pussy tingled and a shiver ran through her as he pushed deeper.

Switching hands and dipping another finger between her lips again to gather more wetness, Richard returned to her ass, stretching the hole wider. To her credit, Lissa did not flinch from his touch; was it possible she enjoyed this as much as he'd hoped she would?

Despite her thoughts, which Richard knew ran just the way he wanted them to, he did not intend to enter her this way. She needed much more preparation than he could give her this morning. Instead, he picked up the small plug he had picked up earlier. Soaking it in her pussy, he then pressed it against her ass until it slid in of its own accord. The small indentation in the end of the plug assured him it would not come out until he was ready to remove it.

"What are you thinking, slave?"

Lissa's deep breathing gave away the state of her need. She tilted her head so she could gasp out her thoughts to her Master. "I feel...full. And I need to come, bad."

"You come only when I allow you to, slave. Do you understand?"

She nodded and tried not to cry out as his fingers once again plunged into her slit and fingered her clit.

"What is it you want, slave?"

"Please, Sir, I want to come. Please let me come!" Desperately she tried to remain still, but the plug in her ass and the torment of his fingers made it almost impossible.

He withdrew his fingers and at first she was afraid he was offended by her begging. But then she realized he stood beside the table, at the lever she had noticed before, but then forgotten. His hand gripped her upper arm as he moved the lever and the table tilted her, head down.

Instinct made her move to catch herself, but her bound hands prevented it. Only his hand around her arm steadied her so she did not slide forward. She heard him lock the table in place, then he came around behind her again, keeping his calming hand on her the whole time.

"You are mine to use as I please. You come when I allow you. What are you thinking?"

Lissa was beyond thought. Her body tingled with anticipation and need, blood rushed to her head and to her upraised pussy. She could only repeat his words to her; words she wrote in the depths of her heart. "I am yours to use as you please; I will come only when you tell me I may."

The last sobbed out of her as his fingers once again danced on her sensitive clit and her pussy throbbed in response. She did not see him remove the towel from his waist; she did not see his magnificent cock as he poised at the entrance to her pussy. She did not see the feral look in his eyes as he pushed on the butt plug, sending a shiver through her.

She moaned in a cry that became a scream as his thick cock plunged deep inside her, pushing her forward despite her attempts to not move. Richard grabbed her bound arms and pulled her up to him, lifting her face from the towel as he impaled her body on his throbbing cock.

"Come for me, slave, let me hear your cries."

Lissa could not hold it in. Her body convulsed with his first words of permission and her muscles contracted around his thickness with the pulses of her orgasm. His hands held her arms and she felt ridden and full and free.

Her spirit soared with his commands and she thrust back onto his shaft, pulling all of him inside as the tingles in her body faded. She was not ready to give this one up.

He felt her push back and knew another orgasm hovered, waiting for him to say the word. The sight of the woman, bound and helpless beneath him, utterly controlled by his word pushed him over the edge and he groaned his command."Come, slave, come with your Master."

Again her muscles contracted, milking him of every drop he had to give her. And when he pulled the plug from her ass, she came again around his cock. Thrust after thrust he pushed his seed deep inside her, forcing her to take his gift to her.

Her cries became whimpers as her body settled, Richard let her down slowly so that her head once more rested on the table. The towel under her head had long slipped to the end of the tilted table; she didn't care. She felt used — well used — and happy.

Richard let her down, but did not move his cock out of her warm nest. Instead, he untied her wrists, massaging her arms as he marveled. All his hard use of her and she did not complain, nor did she use her safeword. Prepared to hear the safeword when he lifted her by her arms, her silence had played a role in his roughness.

Steadying her again, Richard righted the table, giving her back an even surface. He unlocked her ankles from the table and helped her to stand.

Her muscles ached and she felt as if she'd just done fifty pushups. Her pussy felt satisfied as it never had before. Lissa stood before her Master in the morning light and grinned.

"You liked it?" Richard's astonishment shone in his eyes.

"Of course I liked it. No choices, just use. Mutual satisfaction." She eyed his cock, now shrunk in size but still impressive. "You were satisfied, weren't you?"

The look in her eye made him realize she meant more than just the physical aspect of their lovemaking. He gathered her naked body to him and kissed the top of her head.

"Correction, my dear. I *am* satisfied."

* * * * *

David lay with Adora's body entwined in his arms, thinking of his wife. How was Lissa faring this weekend? He checked the clock. Shortly the four of them would be getting together for a late breakfast/early lunch. And a swap of wives again.

He smoothed Adora's hair from her face and glanced down at her peacefulness. No trace of the dominatrix remained. And yet, he disagreed with Richard. Adora had not needed taming, she had needed someone to simply accept her sweetness. With his own demons devouring him, Richard was not the man to enjoy such a "soft" emotion, no matter how much he loved his wife.

And Lissa? She had demons of her own, he now realized. A passion raged in her that was not compatible with his slower and more tender manner. And he missed her.

He had concluded before that it was possible to love two women at the same time—to have his cake and to eat it, too. But did Adora feel the same way? Did Lissa? How did the two women feel about swapping husbands?

Adora sat up, shaking her hair from her face. "It's time we were getting ready." There was a mournful look in her eye, yet a twinkle as well.

"What are you thinking, Adora? About all this?"

"I'm thinking I need not look any further for a man who completes me." She bent down and kissed his lips in a tender embrace.

"And Richard?"

A puzzled look knitted her brows. "What about him?"

"I'm just having some trouble fitting all this together."

She smiled in understanding. "I see. It is not common for four people to be in a marriage together. And yet, that is what we are building. Not one where all four of us live in a house together. But a marriage of sorts in any case."

David considered. Polygamy had been around for centuries, but he'd always thought of it as the man having more than one wife. Why couldn't his wife have more than one husband? One she lived with and one she had sex with? Everything was consensual between and among them.

Or was it? Doubts about Lissa's reaction to Richard lingered. Adora saw his face and guessed what was on his mind.

"I think we will have our answer from them soon. Let's dress and go meet them. We will both know within moments of seeing them if they got along all right."

David nodded and stood to dress, enjoying the view of Adora doing the same. He sincerely hoped it would not be the last time he would ever see her.

* * * * *

Richard ran the water for her shower; nice and hot, just as she liked it. Although he had already bathed, he remained in the bath to hand her into the shower, then stepped in behind her. He was so tall and his shoulders so broad, it seemed he took up the lion's share of the space.

Not that Lissa minded when he took up the soap and lathered it along her sore arms. She flexed each one experimentally. Not any worse than an afternoon spent raking leaves, and infinitely more fun. He turned her shoulders so she faced the water and she let him clean her neck and breasts. The hot water steamed up into her nose and she took a deep breath, leaning against him and relaxing, trusting him to hold her.

His ministrations soft and gentle, he rubbed her body, almost in atonement for his earlier usage of her. She understood and made no attempt to stop him. He made her feel like a whore, and a princess. And when his fingers slipped between her legs to wash away the remnants of their time together, she felt a familiar, comfortable buzz, but no more. She was sated, mind, soul and body.

"We need to leave soon and join Adora and David for lunch." Richard's low baritone murmured in her ear above the rush of water. She started and tried to hide the guilty look on her face. Not once all morning had she even thought of her wonderful husband.

Richard turned off the water and wrapped her in a towel, allowing her to dry herself as he pulled out another one for himself. She wrapped her hair up the same way Adora did, getting it out of her way until she was ready to deal with the tangles.

Neither said much as they dressed. There didn't seem to be much to say. And yet Lissa knew she was bursting with questions. If only she could put them into words. Only when she looked over at Richard and saw him buttoning up another black shirt and her heart skipped a beat all over again, could she begin to articulate some of what she held in her heart.

"Richard," she began, then stopped. Should she call him Master even when they weren't playing? But when were they and when weren't they? She looked at him, the struggle obvious on her face.

Richard saw her distress and crooked his finger at her. Without hesitation, she crossed the small space of the bedroom and stood before him, her hands obediently at her side. He took them in his own, turning them over, running his thumbs along her palms as he sought for words to reassure her.

"Melissa, you are my slave only when we are alone. David will not see you in that light. Perhaps someday he and Adora will join us in our time together, but for the moment, they are content. You have only just shared yourself with me, I do not expect you to share such a deeply held secret with the others yet."

"Thank you for understanding that. Then you don't mind if I call you Richard when we are not...playing?" She knew what the two of them shared was no game, yet no other word seemed to fit.

"Someday, perhaps you will be my total slave, Melissa. But that day is far off. For now we both have spouses we love very much."

She nodded. "Yes, we do." She took a breath and plunged into the thought that consumed her. "Richard, David and I talked about how two people cannot be intimate without their hearts becoming involved. You know he's in love with Adora."

"As she is with him."

"And that's all right with you? You don't mind that my husband loves your wife?"

"I would not have let him spend time with her if I did not think he would love her."

"You know what I mean."

"Yes, Melissa, I do. It bothers me no more than it bothers you that your husband loves another woman."

That stopped her. Lissa thought of David lying in Adora's arms, but no twinge of jealousy arose. She conceded the point.

But the companion point remained between them. The shyness of her nature screamed the question in the privacy of her soul, but she could not bring herself to ask it out loud.

But Richard saw it in her eyes. He pulled her close, wrapping his arms around her slender frame and swallowing her in his embrace. She smelled the cloves of his scent and wrapped her arms around his waist, wanting to hear the words, but afraid to say them first.

"Melissa," he murmured. "No other woman has ever endured what I gave to you and still demanded more of me. You control the demon inside me as no other ever has." He pulled back and looked down at the beautiful woman in his arms. "Even Adora cannot control it. But you do."

Her smile, still melancholy, touched his heart. He understood her fear all too well. To admit what he felt in the depths of his heart was to leave himself open to hurt and shame; a road he had traveled too many times in the past. And yet, the tenderness of her shy gaze could not be denied. He knelt before her, keeping her hands in his.

"I have come to love you, my slave. Because you do not run from me in horror, because you accept what I am and what I need, because you demand more from me, I love you." The Gypsy King bowed to the Slave Girl.

Warmth filled her soul and she knew she would fulfill any command he gave her, at any time he requested it. He loved her and Adora and she loved him and David. Nothing else mattered.

Epilogue

Four people gathered outside the little diner around the corner, looking only a little different from their first meeting: Richard still wore his customary black, but Adora dressed more modestly in a pink sleeveless turtleneck and long skirt. David still wore his khaki pants and white shirt, but Lissa dressed more provocatively, in a low-cut tank top and miniskirt. The women smiled at the irony as they hugged outside the restaurant before going in. Richard leaned down to give Adora a kiss on the cheek and an appreciative wink; David bent over and kissed Lissa's cheek with a small caress on her arm.

The four turned to go into the diner; Lissa and Richard, David and Adora. The little place wasn't too busy; a waitress looked up from the register as they walked in. "How many?"

David looked at their small group and grinned before answering. "Table for four."

About the author:

For many years, Diana Hunter confined herself to mainstream writings. Her interest in the world of dominance and submission, dormant for years, bloomed when she met a man who was willing to let her explore the submissive side of her personality. In her academic approach to learning about the lifestyle, she discovered hundreds of short stories that existed on the topic, but none of them seemed to express her view of a d/s relationship. Challenged by a friend to write a better one, she wrote her first BDSM novel, *Secret Submission*, published by Ellora's Cave Publishing.

Diana welcomes mail from readers. You can write to her c/o Ellora's Cave Publishing at 1337 Commerce Drive, Suite 13, Stow OI I 44224.

Also by Diana Hunter:

Irish Enchantment
Learning Curve
Secret Submission

Why an electronic book?

We live in the Information Age—an exciting time in the history of human civilization in which technology rules supreme and continues to progress in leaps and bounds every minute of every hour of every day. For a multitude of reasons, more and more avid literary fans are opting to purchase e-books instead of paperbacks. The question to those not yet initiated to the world of electronic reading is simply: *why?*

1. *Price.* An electronic title at Ellora's Cave Publishing runs anywhere from 40-75% less than the cover price of the <u>exact same title</u> in paperback format. Why? Cold mathematics. It is less expensive to publish an e-book than it is to publish a paperback, so the savings are passed along to the consumer.

2. *Space.* Running out of room to house your paperback books? That is one worry you will never have with electronic novels. For a low one-time cost, you can purchase a handheld computer designed specifically for e-reading purposes. Many e-readers are larger than the average handheld, giving you plenty of screen room. Better yet, hundreds of titles can be stored within your new library—a single microchip. (Please note that Ellora's Cave does not endorse any specific brands. You can check our website at www.ellorascave.com

for customer recommendations we make available to new consumers.)

3. *Mobility*. Because your new library now consists of only a microchip, your entire cache of books can be taken with you wherever you go.

4. *Personal preferences are accounted for.* Are the words you are currently reading too small? Too large? Too...**ANNOYING**? Paperback books cannot be modified according to personal preferences, but e-books can.

5. *Innovation.* The way you read a book is not the only advancement the Information Age has gifted the literary community with. There is also the factor of what you can read. Ellora's Cave Publishing will be introducing a new line of interactive titles that are available in e-book format only.

6. *Instant gratification.* Is it the middle of the night and all the bookstores are closed? Are you tired of waiting days—sometimes weeks—for online and offline bookstores to ship the novels you bought? Ellora's Cave Publishing sells instantaneous downloads 24 hours a day, 7 days a week, 365 days a year. Our e-book delivery system is 100% automated, meaning your order is filled as soon as you pay for it.

Those are a few of the top reasons why electronic novels are displacing paperbacks for many an avid reader. As always, Ellora's Cave Publishing welcomes your questions and comments. We invite you to email us at service@ellorascave.com or write to us directly at: 1337 Commerce Drive, Suite 13, Stow OH 44224.

Printed in the United States
24663LVS00002B/73-729